Kids in the Wind

Kids in the Wind

Stories

Brad Wethern

 RED HEN PRESS | *Pasadena, CA*

Book design and layout by Michelle Olaya-Marquez
Cover design by Mark E. Cull
Cover image: *Sky Shark Kite* by J. Triepke
(http://creativecommons.org/licenses/by/2.0/legalcode)

Library of Congress Cataloging-in-Publication Data
Wethern, Brad, 1942–
[Short stories. Selections]
Kids in the wind : stories / Brad Wethern.—First edition.
   pages cm
ISBN 978-1-59709-419-1 (pbk.)
I. Title.
PS3623.E8845A6 2015
813'.6—dc23
                    2014037138

The National Endowment for the Arts, the Los Angeles County Arts Commission, the Los Angeles Department of Cultural Affairs, the Dwight Stuart Youth Fund, the Pasadena Arts & Culture Commission and the City of Pasadena Cultural Affairs Division, the Ahmanson Foundation, and Sony Pictures Entertainment partially support Red Hen Press.

First Edition
Published by Red Hen Press
www.redhen.org

Acknowledgments

I would first like to thank the pals of my Fairhaven childhood for providing me with such rich memories and for the brief moments of literary recognition created by the teacher at the two-room schoolhouse (Rolph School), Ms. Naida Olsen Gipson.

And more recently, I would also like to thank Maia Donadee, for her love, inspirational help and incredibly insightful editing support in writing this work.

And, of course, the fast-paced mind of Patty Powers for mentorship dinners and brainstorming powwows.

And Dr. Patt Perkins, of the Claremont Center for Spiritual Living, for her insightful spiritual support.

And I want to thank the indomitable Dr. Daniel Duroseau, international worker in faith and teeth, and Sung Shin, unsung literary aficionado, for the special encouragement each gave during the writing and preparation of my work.

And of course, there is the much-published Dr. Don Marshall, professor of English, a high school friend (BFF) I rediscovered after nearly a lifetime.

And Ernest Joselovitz, also a classmate from South Gate High, long gone and then returned, who found his literary perch as a world-class playwright.

And my kids, Mark and Heather, their mother, Elizabeth and my parents, Frankie and Ronn, all of whom added the layers of benign craziness to my canon.

And June and Bob Reddick, friends and financial planners, who exclaimed "Incredible!" when they first read the book.

And everyone at the Claremont Center and all my real estate buddies who tolerate my right-brain way of being and doing business. Noteworthy of which are the Ruchs, whose long friendship I cherish.

And Virginia Moreno, who sat up with me years ago editing my first novel, who always said that my writing was up there with Steinbeck and that if I had stayed with her I would be a millionaire now.

And Deena Metzger, whose workshops of quiet understanding I attended many years ago when I was first developing my crazy sense of awareness.

And all the kind and generous folks from Minnesota. You betcha.

And Jackson Burgess, writer and professor at Berkeley, in whose class I wrote a story that won the Julia Keith Shrout Short Story Prize one year.

There are many others, family and friends, who have come in and out my door over the years, who have added to the texture of this American life. I am grateful to you all.

Brad Wethern
Ontario, California

This book is dedicated to my two great kids

Mark and Heather

Contents

Preface

THESE STORIES ARE FICTION, I think. They are created from the memories and constructs of a lifetime lived as a former child. I would like to acknowledge all the kids and all the adults I encountered during these years who provided such a rich supply of experience to ponder and write about.

Childhood memories are selective. No two kids will remember the same events or recall shared events in the same way. It is said that the history of the world is written by the victors. Likewise the history of childhood is written by the survivors. In this collection of short stories, childhood is filled with fantasy, reality, kid ideas, humor, and moral codes that are far from fully formed. Welcome to the world of the Flying Boxcar and some kids in the wind.

A Passage to Fairhaven

THE WORLD OF THE GRAMMAR SCHOOL is familiar to most people. The world of Fairhaven on the north spit of Humboldt Bay in the 1950s is familiar to very few.

In order to understand the little settlement of Fairhaven, you need to know that it is a strip of land that juts out from the Northern California coast, surrounding the north half of Humboldt Bay. Until a seaplane base was built at the very tip of the peninsula during World War II, there was no highway going to it. The primary means of access was to arrive by boat or cross the bay by ferry from Eureka.

Fairhaven was originally occupied by the Weott Indians who were the victims of a massacre in the 1860s. Arrowheads could still be found beneath the lupines in the 1950s, but there were no Weott Indians around.

There were a few families that lived there and then in the 1950s, a subdivision was created and individual lots were sold to those who wished to settle there, many so they could walk to work at the always busy Mutual Plywood Mill.

There were no building codes that anyone seemed to know about. The terms of sale on the lots were so close to "nothing down and nothing a month" that it made it easy for nearly anyone to qualify. As a result, many of the houses were tarpaper shacks and had outdoor plumbing. They all had water, because you could reach clear water by digging four feet and putting in a pitcher pump. All had electricity because there were REA power poles nearby. However, there were no telephones, there was no TV, and most significantly there was no law that was readily available. The police came seventeen miles around the peninsula from Eureka. There were some conventional homes there, (former Governor Rolph's once stylish previous home was one) but they were becoming the minority as the low-end lot sales boomed.

It was a place of daily wind and stormy weather with sand dunes and lupine bushes everywhere. The sandy roads were covered liberally with large plywood chips, made at the mill, which came out of a giant wood chipper known as the Hog. It made good cheap roads, and everyone called it hog fuel.

John and Marnie

OF THE TWENTY-FIVE FIRST GRADERS in Mrs. Mann's class, just about everyone had something they learned that no one else could do. One guy could burp any time he wanted. By the end of the first week he had four followers who could do the same. Another guy, probably from out of state, could touch the bridge of his nose with his tongue. He tried to teach some of us, but after a few minutes we saw there wasn't anything to learn. He just had, in addition to a very long tongue, a very long nose. And one guy could shoot big rubber bands with only one hand. Load and shoot. Load and shoot. He was fast and accurate, but he didn't want to teach anybody. He said it was more fun shooting them.

There was a very thin girl who could do cartwheels all the way up one aisle and all the way down the next without ever stopping or touching a desk. She took tumbling classes and wore special underwear. The girl I liked was the one who could pull a button off your shirt and sew it back on, because she had a needle and thread in her lunch pail.

I didn't know it at the time, but it would be only a matter of two or three years before the unique skills that defined our first grade personae would be all but forgotten. That is with one exception and that was the remarkable talent of John and Marnie.

I assumed they were neighbors. They would usually walk to and from school together and even sat in seats next to each other. They were very polite, both wore nice clothes, spoke with quiet voices (you could hardly hear either one of them unless you were right next to them) and they didn't like to trade sandwiches so they would usually eat by themselves. During lunchtime activities Marnie would jump rope and laugh with the girls and John was very fast and reliable when we played tag and Red Rover. On their own they got along just fine and fit into whatever was happening as good as any of us first graders could. But together, as a team, they became the most enchanting, charismatic and unbelievable pair of six-year-olds alive. John and Marnie did one thing probably better than anyone in the whole world. They could kiss just like Hollywood stars at the end of a movie.

The first time I saw them do it, I thought I was dreaming. They looked just like real movie stars when they put their arms around each other, leaned just a little, closed their eyes, came together and then held it just like that. The end.

"Wow," I said. "It looked so real."

They both thanked me so quietly I barely caught the words as kids came running in the room, out of breath from tag and ball playing. Lunch was nearly over.

"You've got to see this," I told them. "Would you do that thing again?" I asked John and Marnie.

"Okay," they said and they did it again. When they were through, the small group was motionless.

"How did you learn to do it?" someone asked.

"We just did it one day and practiced," Marnie said.

More kids began filling the room, laughing and hitting. Nearly the whole class was there.

"Could you do it for everybody?" someone asked.

"Okay," they said.

"Watch. This is very good," I said.

A circle formed around them and some of those in the back stood on tables and desks.

"What are they going to do?" someone asked.

"Just watch. There is no way to say it," I said.

"Everybody ready?" John asked. A group "uh-huh" brushed the air. They embraced and kissed just the way they had before only this time they held it for an even longer time. If they weren't so short, you'd swear they were getting married. The usual hoots and whistles were absent. No eyes moved. No one made a sound. The moment was so perfect; I think I came alive inside for the first time in my life. I knew for sure I wouldn't be a kid forever. There was an adult in me somewhere, just waiting for exactly the right instant to come shooting out.

Mrs. Mann first appeared pushing the door with her shoe. She marched straight ahead, carrying a large carton of books with her purse on top.

"Everyone is so quiet. It's a real pleasure to come into a room that is . . ." She was putting the carton on her desk and turned to smile at everyone. Instead, she made a sound I never heard before or since. "Whoa ho! Whoa ho!" I thought of Santa trying to stop his reindeer and say "Ho ho ho!" at the same time.

John and Marnie were just finishing and no one paid attention to Mrs. Mann as she crossed the room. Most of the girls were smiling or leaning their heads to the side and the boys were looking like they had just seen Casper the friendly ghost.

"Stop stop stop. Stop stop stop stop, stop! What in the name of God's green earth is happening here?" she yelled.

John and Marnie came apart slowly, their eyes still on each other. They stood side by side and looked up at Mrs. Mann as if they expected her to say "I now pronounce you husband and wife." But she didn't. Instead she separated them by wriggling her fingers in between where their shoulders were touching. Without ever taking her eyes off them, she called to the rest of us. "Lunch is over. Back to your seats, now!"

The moment was gone; the air seemed cold and the room smelled funny. No one spoke. John and Marnie, uncharacteristic of the Movietone celebrities they portrayed so perfectly, had to go to the principal's office. Mrs. Mann spoke to the rest of us in her deepest, gruffest, story-telling voice. The one she normally reserved for the villains and large, hostile animals. No one was to ever do that again in the school. Ever. Period. Okay? No one reacted. She looked puzzled for a little bit and then asked if anyone was awake. Was she going to have to go around the room and make each one of us promise? The tension shattered as laughter filled the room. She wanted to know what was so amusing.

A girl stood up quickly and said, "You don't have make us promise. There aren't any two kids in the school who would do that for all the money in the bank. Even if they could."

She sat down and another girl stood up immediately. "And nobody could either. Because they did something really different. It was like an oil painting or a fancy dance."

"It certainly was," Mrs. Mann said. "And that should make it easy to remember that there are three things we don't do in the first grade. Oil painting, fancy dancing and that." The word "that" sent a flat echo across the valley of braids and cowlicks.

It was time for the afternoon story. Heads dropped forward, Mrs. Mann reached for the book and began reading. Somewhere in the middle of the adventure, complete with special voices, the sound of the wind over the mountains and even tree noises, John and Marnie pushed the door to the classroom open together. They walked back into the room single file and quietly took their seats across from each other. Mrs. Mann saw them, but pretended not to and continued reading brilliantly without missing a phrase, a voice, a waterfall or even the lowly sound of a stump.

Everyone's head was down, but I shifted around so I could see between the desks. They were sitting up. Marnie's back was toward me, but I caught a glimpse of John just as they turned to look at each other. The back of his hands had red marks across them and I could see he had been crying.

Afternoon of the Bully

IT HAD STOPPED RAINING in plenty of time for recess, but there were mud puddles everywhere. The playground was like a huge assortment of chocolates. They were creamy and thick, big, small, pale, dark, some swirling, some bumpy and some so smooth the rays of the sun seemed to cover them with gold foil.

The new, tall boy was swinging on the big swings, standing up and going so high that for one lightning second we could see his full-length reflection in the large puddle under him like a giant statue that was falling to earth. As the swing passed close to the ground, Hugh Talor suddenly grabbed the new boy's nearest ankle. The boy lost his balance, dropped to one knee on the wooden seat and spun out of control. He got tangled in the chains, and banging against the uprights, he hit his head and started bleeding a little. He then dropped onto the seat so he straddled it while he dragged his feet and came to a muddy stop.

"Are you crazy?" the new boy asked.

"You better shut up, chocolate boy," Hugh Talor said.

Because he was new, I had never seen the boy's face up close. He was very dark. Now I knew there were other kinds of people in the world besides those we had in Oregon. I had seen pictures of some working on railroads. They were the Chinese. I had seen some on horseback riding in front of the cavalry. They were the Indians. And as far as the naked ones I saw in National Geographic every month? I just knew them as natives. And I knew about Eskimos, of course, but they stayed inside their fur hoods most of the time so I never did know exactly what they looked like. In the second grade that was just about my complete knowledge of the types of human beings.

This new boy fit into no category I knew of. He was tall and thin with very short hair and a strong nose. He was different all right, but so were most lumberjacks or the waitresses at the pancake house.

"You shouldn't call people names," the new boy said.

"Why not?" Hugh asked.

"Because it's, well, it's ignorant," the new boy said.

"You're calling me ignorant? Shut up!" Hugh said. "I'll knock you from here to next week."

"Are you challenging me? Do you want to spar?" the new boy asked.

"Spar? I don't know what that means. What's your name anyway?"

"Bucyrus," the boy said.

Hugh Talor laughed. "You know what I want? I don't want you playing on these swings no more."

"I can play on the swings just like everyone else," Bucyrus said.

"Not while I'm here you can't. You are dark and dirty and you get everything dirty. I don't like you. Nobody in my family likes you. You either go to another school by tomorrow or I'll person-ally scare you so bad you'll turn white. Then I'll be a hero." Hugh Talor was talking more than I ever heard him. He was usually punching, cursing or taking somebody's money.

"You are a bully and bullies are cowards, not heroes," Bucyrus said. "And heroes can die only once, but a coward dies a thousand times."

A lot more than a cat, I thought, but I didn't say anything.

Hugh Talor chanted as he danced around the swing, slapping Bucyrus on the head and chest.

Bucyrus finally screamed back at him. "Crazy old white boy!"

A nearsighted yard teacher ran over to stop the commotion.

"He's calling me names," Hugh Talor said.

The yard teacher told Bucyrus that name-calling was not tol-erated at the school. He looked over the top of his thick glasses and told him to go wash up his face. Bucyrus shook his head and walked toward the boy's room.

When he had gone, Hugh Talor got a group around him and told them that we couldn't allow the new boy to stay in school. "If you let one in, pretty soon the whole school will be dark." He said that his dad was a lineman, which he said was like a cowboy only with wire cutters instead of a gun. His dad had to work with dark people like this now, and they had driven him to drink, which he had done on his own anyway, but now it was worse. Someone wanted to know what was so bad about them.

"Well, they are dark and they are too tall and they talk funny. Didn't you notice?" Hugh asked. "And wherever they go, every-thing gets worse. And pretty soon there are going to be more of them."

"There can't be too many," I said. "He's the first one I ever saw."

Hugh Talor walked over to me and stood on both of my feet. He held my jacket so I wouldn't fall over.

"Do you have any money?" he asked.

"No," I said.

"Then shut up!"

"Okay," I said. "I can bring some tomorrow if you get off my feet."

"Do that," he said and let me go. *This wasn't my fight. I wasn't the sheriff,* I thought, but I didn't say anything.

Shopping that afternoon with my mother, I looked around town for more people like Bucyrus, but there weren't any in Corvallis that I could see. I told my mother what Hugh Talor had said. She said there were no chocolate people. Just like there were no vanilla people or strawberry people or lemon people. It sounded pretty obvious when she said it that way. People aren't ice cream. People are just people and everyone is different, she added. She wanted to know if Hugh Talor was a bully. He sounded like one. I told her he hit people, called them names, and took their money.

"Did he hit you or take your money?" she asked.

"Not yet," I said. "I was going to bring him some tomorrow."

"No you aren't," she said.

"Okay," I said. "What do I do when he pounds me? He says money is poison and it's his job to hit people to beat the poison out of them."

"I will go to the school and talk to your teacher," she said.

I didn't know if she did. Things seemed to be about the same the next day. I didn't have any money so Hugh Talor shoved me into the bushes just before the same nearsighted yard teacher came by and told me to use the boy's room next time or he would send me to the principal.

In Geography, the teacher told us Bucyrus had just moved here from another part of the world. He was of a different race, but we should treat him the same. She asked him what his racial origin was. He said he thought the human race. She said that was right, but she wanted something more specific.

Hugh Talor whispered to his friends, "The chocolate race," but only a few kids laughed.

"What is your actual origin?" she asked.

"I'm Egyptian," he said.

"Don't you mean African?" she asked.

"Egypt is in Africa," he said and pointed to the map.

"You are right," the teacher said. "That's enough geography for today. It's lunchtime. Hugh, I want to see you before you go out. Everyone else dismissed."

Maybe my mother did come to school.

That afternoon as we started home from class, Hugh Talor didn't bother anybody for once. He growled a little, walking with his eyes looking around at kids, but he didn't hit anybody or take their money or call anyone names. Then he saw a figure up on a power pole as we reached the corner where the crossing guard stood.

"That's my dad," he said. Everyone looked around, but they didn't see anybody. Then they looked up and saw a lineman. He was waving down at Hugh Talor with one hand.

"Watch this, dad!" Hugh said and he suddenly started punching Bucyrus who started punching him back to defend himself. While they were occupied with that, several kids started screaming so Hugh stopped and looked up the tall pole with the rest of them. The lineman had lost his balance and accidently grabbed a live wire to keep from falling. His hand was still holding it and his body was moving around like he was still alive, but I knew he wasn't. *I just knew it.*

The crossing guard and several teachers started herding everyone back inside. They tried to make us look away, but they couldn't grab everybody's head at the same time. The face of

Hugh Talor's dad was brown, almost black and there was still more sparks of electricity going through him.

We stayed in the room for over an hour while they got him down. We were supposed to be reading, but we couldn't. When we finally were allowed to leave the classroom, we walked past where Hugh Talor was slumped, bumping his head slowly against his desk. Some kids tried to say they were sorry, but Hugh tried to hit them with his head still down.

"Leave him alone," the teacher said. "Please."

There was nothing much I could think to say anyway. I never thought I would see Hugh Talor cry and now it seemed like he couldn't stop. The top of his desk had pools of wet all over it. *Dark puddles from all the poisons coming out of him*, I thought.

A Pledge of Allegiance

Moving to a new school in the middle of the second grade is like playing 52 Pickup with all your people and things. When you try to collect them and put them back together, you can't, because they are somebody else's people now and somebody else's things.

@

"**I PLEDGE ALLEGIANCE TO THE FLAG** of the United States of America and to the republic for which it stands. One nation, indivisible, with liberty and justice for all. Someone can tell Lance to come back in now," the teacher said.

"Me."

"Me."

"Me me me!"

"Whose turn is it?"

"Me."

"Me."

"No, Me. Me. ME!"

"Okay. You."

"Me?"

"You."

"Me! Yeaay!" said the winning messenger. "Run run run. I mean walk walk walk. You can come back in now.... Lance? He's not here. Oh, there you are, behind the door. We're all through with the flag salute, Lance."

Before I sat down again, I checked my shoes and under my seat to find out where the smell of paste was coming from. The messenger returned to her seat followed by a well-groomed boy. He had on a V-neck sweater, maroon; and corduroys, blue; and shoes, shiny oxblood; and hair, perfect. Somebody must have dressed him and carried him to school. But why did they have him in the hall? It was something I didn't understand, and now I was afraid to sit down, because I had discovered where the smell was coming from. I had paste on my pants.

In the days that followed, I learned to move slowly and watch carefully. The teacher, Miss Klopenstein—I couldn't pronounce her name at first—would always smile a phony smile and say, "Good morning. Would the class please rise?" And then she would stop smiling abruptly and say, "Lance, you can go out in the hall now. Someone will call you when we are through." Her eyes would follow him like a camera covering a big newsreel event. The world is astounded. The king's kid walks out on the flag salute. I didn't know why Lance was excused each day, but when he returned, his face seemed to have a grownup glaze, which protected him from the squinty regard Miss Klopenstein always had for him. His reason for leaving, whatever it was, seemed to be serious and essential. Like vaccinations and bomb drills, which were two other things I didn't really understand.

But I had other serious things to deal with. For instance, paste could show up anywhere at the worst time. And I wasn't familiar with any of the textbooks we were using at this school. The spelling workbook was so tricky, with its games and puzzlers, I couldn't find the spelling words themselves. And the numbers in the arithmetic book must have been designed at night by a mad doctor. The fives, the sixes, and the nines all had warts on their ends. The sevens had big shingles. The ones had little platforms as well as big shingles, and the zeros had grown tall and thin like bean stalks.

I was studying and scratching where the paste had gone through my pants and dried, trying to keep it from turning into permanent glue.

"Is everything all right here? Do you have any questions?" Miss Klopenstein was standing right over me. I asked if the numbers in the arithmetic book were the same numbers I had been adding and subtracting at my last school. She squinted at me like she did at Lance, and then leaned over to get a closer look at what I was talking about.

"Those? Yes, of course. Numbers are numbers. Anywhere you go."

"Anywhere I go?" I accidentally said it too loud, trying to make her hair go away from my face. She snapped back up and continued to look at me, then at the paste on my pants.

"Yes yes yes! Always the same. Anywhere you go." She leaned over again, breathing deeply and whispering in my ear. "And speaking of going, did you go in your pants?"

"No. I got paste on my pants and now it's stuck on my pants," I whispered back.

"Paste washes out. That's all you need to know about paste. Arithmetic is more important. Not only do you have to learn it, it touches everything we do here at school."

"Paste does too."

"Well, it's not supposed to. Is there anything else on your mind before I start back to my desk?"

"There's something worries me," I said. She squinted and leaned down once again. "Why does Lance have to go out in the hall?" I asked. She straightened up like an old, island lighthouse, her eyes scanning the room with a nautical sweep of her beam, denying two raised hand emergencies, while uncovering an entire funny book smuggling ring and a live garter snake. "Lance doesn't *have* to go out in the hall for the flag salute," she said. "It's his choice."

Lance looked over when he heard his name. The teacher ignored him, making a sudden octopus sweep up and down the aisles. She snagged the snake from a student in one hand and without stopping, shushed everyone who had an emergency, then scooped up several funny books in the other hand and studied the covers on the way back to her desk. She put the funny books on her desktop and shut the garter snake in the lower right hand drawer. It made a rattling sound as it moved around other things in the drawer.

◉

The morning recess was another big change for me. They called it nutrition. It was no longer an activity. It was a food. So instead of shouting "*Geronimo!*" and running full speed toward the nearest piece of playground equipment, we stayed at our desks while the nutrition monitor came with milk. If someone needs to go to the boys' room or girls' room, this was the time the teacher allowed them to go without getting personal. But we could only go one at a time, and only with the hall pass and special key.

At my old school we didn't need hall passes. The principal could tell if you were up to no good just by looking at you. No keys either. There wasn't any door; just an L-shaped tin wall. You walked to the left and walked to the right, hit the tin to announce your arrival and there you were. And it better be the correct side, because if you accidentally ran into the girls' side by mistake, your only hope was to drop to the floor, guard the family jewels, and scramble out while you still had both eyes in your head.

The nutrition monitor had a crayon name tag that said "MONITOR" as well as a tray with a small carton of milk and a fresh straw for everyone in the room. Everyone who had paid, that is. I sat quietly the first day and listened to kids talking and milk flowing all around me. I remembered part of a poem. "Water water water everywhere and not a drop to drink." There were sounds and voices. Up, down, gurgle, blip. Not out your nose! How did he do that! The girl in front of me craned her rubber neck around so she looked right at me and said with a milky spray "If you get caught blowing bubbles, they will take you off the milk program."

"I don't know how to get *on* the milk program," I said.

When everyone was through, the teacher stood in front of her desk, clapping twice every so often to quiet everyone and then trying to speak in between like a talking seal. She was sorry I didn't get any milk. (Clap clap) If I wanted some tomorrow, (Clap clap) I needed to bring money.

"I have money now," I said and clapped twice.

"Why are you clapping? And I can barely hear you," she said. (Clap clap) "Quiet, please! I can't hear him. Oh you have money now. Oh, I didn't know that." (Clap clap) "That's good. Just bring it again tomorrow, okay? Nutrition is over now. Let's settle down, pupils." She was waving the hall pass over her head. "Last call for down the hall," she barked. The brass key glistened from the sunlight outside.

"Who needs to use this next?" Hands went up, but she offered me first dibs. The students' faces, connected to the flying hands, were anxiously awaiting my decision. Why did she think the one person in the room who didn't get a drink would need to use the toilet first? I shook my head for no. The faces all cheered. It was a crazy school, but it wasn't hard to be a hero.

@

That afternoon we went outside for what they called physical education. It sounded good at first, but on the way to the playground, all the girls vanished. The rest of us were waiting in line to see how far we could kick a volleyball. I asked the guy in front of me if there was a game we would kick the volleyball in.

"Volley Kickball," he said.

"What's that?" I asked.

"It's like Hit-Pin-Kickball, only there's no pins, and you use a volleyball," he said.

"I never played it," I said.

"That's because you're new. I think they invented it here, but they never bothered telling anybody outside the school. It's actually more like sock ball, or dodgeball only you use your foot instead of your hand, but you still run around the bases and they try to tag you out at home."

"Like baseball," I said.

"I guess it is," he said, "but I don't know that much about sports. I know more about dogs and crime."

I asked him about Dobermans. He said they were mean. He got that right so I asked him why Lance left the room during the flag salute. He said that I better not ask it too loud if the teacher was around. She didn't like the Lance deal one bit. What deal? I wanted to know.

"Lance is a witness," he whispered excitedly close to my head. A sour mist settled in my ear. Milk was worse than paste, because when it got warm on some kids it smelled like puke.

"A witness?" I was rubbing my ear to get the milk out. "What do you mean?"

"You don't know what a witness is?" he asked.

"Sure. It's somebody who saw something bad and lived to tell about it."

"It's more than that," he said.

"Jeez! What did he see?" I asked.

"Who knows?" he said.

"Well, I sure don't," I said. "I'm new. Remember?"

"He probably didn't see nothin'," he said. "Because he's not a regular witness. He's a Jova witness."

"Jova? J-O-V-A? What's that?"

"It's a different kind of witness, but don't laugh. There's a bunch of them. And they are serious."

He told me that Jova Witnesses all had a funny feeling that something important happened, and they might have seen it, so they dressed up every day in case they had to go to court to testify. But nobody wanted them in court, because they didn't see anything. But they didn't care. They still wanted to be witnesses. They even knocked on doors to get more witnesses. But a lot of the people saw how nice they looked and thought they were selling something so they always tried to slam the door on their foot. The police didn't want them and the judges didn't want them. Even the accident lawyers didn't want them. So they took to sitting around trying to witness each other. But after a while it got so boring; they were hoping and praying that something would happen. Anything. Then one day, one of them jumped up with an idea. "Hey, as long as we're hopin' and prayin', we might as well be a church!" And somebody else jumped up and said "Then we'll have some place to wear our new clothes!" Pretty soon everybody jumped up and down and that's how they got the Jova Witness Church.

The line wasn't moving anywhere near as fast as his story was. I looked to the front and saw why. Two boys and the coach were trying to put more air in the ball.

"Do you wonder what Jova means?" he asked me.

"No," I said. "I just heard it."

"I think it means some kind of coffee. That's how they got woke up to be Jova witnesses. Lance said the word Jova was in the Bible, but somebody said they looked and it wasn't there. Lance said not anymore, because the Bible was written in sand script a long time ago, and a lot of it blew away."

The volleyball was hard and rolling again. The line began to move, but I still didn't learn about Lance and the flag salute.

"Okay. I'll say it short. Lance told the teacher he didn't have to do the flag salutes, but the teacher said he did, so his parents said they were going to hire a thorty. That's when the school board got scared and had a secret meeting. Now Lance doesn't have to do the flag salute."

"What's a thorty?"

"It's like a Jova witness lawyer, I think. Instead of hiring a lawyer, you hire a thorty. That's why Lance got his way. Who wants to go to court with a hired thorty and that many witnesses against you," he said.

It was his turn to kick the ball. He asked me if I wanted to go first. I said sure. He was my first friend. His name was Jim.

Every morning I watched Lance go out. One day he stopped and told the teacher that she didn't have to call out his name to leave anymore. He knew when to go out and he didn't mind do-ing it without being asked. He could count exactly how long it took to say the pledge now, so he could come back in at the right time without having somebody come and get him.

After that day, when the teacher asked everyone to rise for the Pledge of Allegiance, she would press her lips together and look at the ceiling like she was waiting to kiss an old person. But she didn't get to do it long, because Lance would always be up automatically and on his way to the door. Once, she tried to pretend she was wiping her nose, and then said it real fast to catch him off guard. She did, too. Just once. After that, Lance started walking out the second she said good morning. No matter how fast she tried to talk, by the time she asked us to rise, Lance was long gone.

She always placed her hand high on her chest and looked around to see if we did the same. "Right over your heart," she would say. My doctor told me that if her heart was up there, she would choke to death. My friend, Jim, said she wasn't worried. Because she didn't have one.

@

A few days later, the teacher wanted to have us elect a person for a new monitor position. Paste monitor. When she said what the new position was, nobody wanted to run. It was a sticky job. Finally, she nominated Lance. My new friend, Jim, nominated me for a practical joke to see my reaction. He laughed, and whispered to everybody to vote for Lance. We covered our eyes with one hand and voted with the other, and Lance won. I was relieved. Jim and I shook hands, smiling at each other.

Then Lance stood up and said: "I didn't want to run, I didn't shut my eyes, and I don't want the job. Thank you."

My heart stopped. Thanks to my friend's joke, I was the new paste monitor.

The teacher asked if I wanted to say anything to the class about winning the election.

"Yes," I said, "I do. Everyone has to turn in your paste to me today."

During Nutrition that day, we had a visit from the big fat principal who said she had a special announcement.

"Would everyone please stop the sucking noise with your milk for a minute? Thank you. There will be no spelling today."

Everyone cheered.

"Wait!" she said, but it was too late. Milk cartons were flying. The principal looked at the teacher sternly. "That's not the announcement. Now pick up your cartons! This is the announcement. The Congress has voted to change the flag salute. They have added two new words and out of habit, they put them in the middle so they wouldn't be noticed that much until it was too late. But this time, they didn't hide them well enough so we are taking time out today from spelling to practice saying the flag salute in the new way to be ready for Monday when the change takes place. Are there any questions?"

Everyone's hand went up. "Here is the person to answer them! Let's welcome, a new student teacher, Miss Angle!"

A white dress flowed in the door. Inside it was a pretty young woman who was going to teach us the new flag salute.

"Hi Miss Angel!" everyone said.

She wrinkled her nose for everyone and said "Hi! It's really Miss Angle, hard G, but you can call me Miss Angel if it's easier to remember." She went from one side of the room to the other, waving and winking like a crazy princess from a fairy tale book.

Why couldn't we get a teacher like this? I thought, as the big fat principal switched a few flies with her hair as she turned in place and settled into a horse trot out the classroom door.

Miss Angle was the perfect person to teach the flag salute. She had little blue eyes and lipstick all over her front teeth. Red, white and blue.

"Okay, everyone in Happy Land, let's start. Okay?"

"Okay!" we all shouted.

"Okay. Let's start with the two new words first. All by themselves. Not with anything else, okay?"

"Okay!" we shouted.

"Now the two words are, well, the first one is 'God,' and the second one is 'under.' But not in that order. You probably want to have God first, that's the way I was brought up, but in this case He's after 'under.'"

"What?" we all shouted.

"God's after 'under' here," she said.

"What!" my friend said. "God's after our underwear?"

Everyone put their hand over their mouth laughing.

Miss Klopenstein was looking out the window, rolling her eyes, when she suddenly spun around, remembering something.

"Sorry to interrupt. Forgive me. Lance! I think you better go out in the hall. It will be a little longer this time. Just wait until we call you."

Lance stood and started to say something, but the teacher said, "Go go go. We're on a schedule here. You are holding up the entire class." Lance turned and walked out of the room.

"Why is he leaving the room?" Miss Angle wanted to know. Miss Klopenstein shook her head and walked back to the window without speaking. Miss Angle looked at her with her eyebrows going up and down almost to her hairline and back.

She could teach flag raising too.

Miss Klopenstein shook her head more and motioned for her to continue.

"He's a communist? An atheist?" Miss Angle asked.

The teacher squeezed her eyes tight and turned toward the wall, holding up her two crossed index fingers.

"He's possessed?"

"Never mind!" Miss Klopenstein shouted. Everyone jumped.

It took a long time for all of us to get the extra words "under God" in the right place at the right time in the right way. After fifteen minutes, Lance opened the door, and our teacher told him we weren't through yet.

"But I . . ." he started to say.

"Not now! Lance!"

A few minutes later he did it again. Then again.

"Stop it, Lance! Stop it!" the teacher screamed. "Just because you don't salute the flag, doesn't mean you have to ruin the country for the rest of us!"

Miss Angle stuck her finger in her ear like her eardrum had been shattered. Everyone laughed. Even Miss Klopenstein laughed.

"I'm sorry," Miss Klopenstein apologized, still smiling. "But enough is enough. He doesn't have to pledge allegiance, but I have to draw the line somewhere. He is just going to have to show some common decency. We have our priorities, too!"

By the time we could all say it twice in a row with no mistakes, an hour had passed. Miss Angle's lipstick was all gone. Wherever lipstick goes. There was none on her teeth, none anywhere. She thanked us as we stood and clapped and waved good-bye, following her out the door as she turned down the hall.

"Oh, no!" she said and turning to a place behind the door. Lance was kneeling on the floor, facing the classroom wall. His eyes were unfocused, and his hands were together between his knees. The floor all around him was wet. Miss Angle kneeled and spoke to him. He closed his eyes and didn't move. She lifted him up over her shoulder. Yellow was staining her white dress as she carried him slowly down the hall. Lance's head rolled against her neck, his face was red, and his navy blue pants were soaked. She talked to him as we watched silently from the classroom door.

◉

Lance wasn't at school the next day. Neither was Miss Klopenstein. We had substitutes for two weeks before she returned from what she called a leave of absence, which sounded phony right away, because if you leave, naturally you're absent. She said she was making some changes in the monitor system. After she made me return everyone's paste, there would no longer be a paste monitor.

Fine with me.

Also, we would begin having a member of the class lead the flag salute, and it was to be me. I was to become the first flag monitor. There would be no election. It was what she called an appointed position. She even wrote it on the board. It's what she called 50-cent words.

"Where is Lance?" I asked.

"None of your beeswax," she answered, and we never saw him again.

◉

For the rest of my public school days, no one ever left the room during the flag salute. Not even foreign exchange students with flags of their own back home. I always wondered if putting "under God" in the middle had anything to do with it. I never found out, but it didn't matter. After a time no one even remembered that "under God" had ever been added. We took our turns leading the flag salute during my next ten years of education at the grammar schools in Oregon and Northern California, and later the large high school when we moved to Los Angeles. When I led the Pledge of Allegiance, I couldn't help remembering Lance being carried away by Miss Angle.

Sometimes somebody would mention that I led the flag salute very well and I would think they were kidding me, but by the time I was in high school, I noticed I was leading the flag salute an incredible number of times. No one led the flag salute as much as I did. No one wanted to, including me. It was like an embarrassing millstone around my regular guy persona. It was like having a second career before I had a first one. Then it started getting out of hand. The Rotary Club was calling. The Chamber of Commerce. I was getting excused from classes to go to community luncheons. There was Boy's Day at City Hall. Celebrity Dinners. I was always sitting at the head table, right next to the guest of honor, eating free food.

Fine with me.

One night at an event, the mayor wanted to know what I did besides lead a great flag salute.

"Not much," I told him. "The flag salute's about it."

He put his hand on my shoulder and looked right into my eyes. "Me too. Only don't tell the city council," he said with a straight face. "I'll deny everything!" Then he laughed and offered me a summer job. I accepted, but two months later he lost his bid for re-election and was looking for a job himself.

I led the Pledge of Allegiance for the last time at high school graduation. When the silver-haired principal handed me my diploma, she whispered "Masterful. Once again. The way you get everyone on their feet and look across the whole crowd before starting." I think she was just supposed to say a quick word or two, because they kept reading the graduates' names while she talked to me and the graduates, who were supposed to stay arms distance apart, started bunching up closer together. She continued, "Even with a group this big, you could hear a pin drop when you started. That pause always makes me a little nervous, but your timing is perfect. Congratulations. Omigod!" The roll readers had already called many more names than people had come forward, and the line had backed up so much that the graduates were stepping on each other's robes. Pomp, circumstance, and the stepping on rayon were the last sounds I remember of that day.

❧

I was obsolete by nightfall. In the morning, it was like I had just transferred to the new school back in the second grade. Only now the new school was called the world. Everywhere I went my friends and familiar things seemed to be drifting away. They became somebody else's people now and somebody else's things. And for the rest of my life I never led the flag salute again. But if I did, I'd do it the same way I did during those school days. Once everyone was standing, I would always take a long pause, giving Lance plenty of time to leave before I began.

Family Fishing— Fairhaven Style

I ALWAYS LIKED TO FISH. Ever since whenever. We fished in a stream behind our house in Oregon. Family fished, don't you know. Picnic lunch. Mother. Father. Brother. Sister. Big can of worms. At the edge of the apple orchard, I had my favorite spot in the tall grass where I felt safe and secure.

We caught wriggly little fish that we would sometimes throw back because they were too small. It was a big decision for little people. Life and death. Food or freedom. How big is not small? Keep or give back? How could I make such a quick choice, when it was forever? Mom! Dad! They are clear downstream. By the time they come and say too small, you'll be dead. I don't know. Back you go. Hey, I think he turned and thanked me. I wonder if that's possible. Okay, everybody! Who took the worms? I want to catch a really big one now. That's family fishing.

ⓔ

Later, when I was eleven years old and we lived on Humboldt Bay, we fished from a large, L-shaped dock in Fairhaven where two commercial salmon boats were sometimes tied. I fished with older kids, just after low tide with big lines, big hooks and giant mudworms we dug at dawn from the kelp beds. We fished for movie money. We needed big poles with long handles and star drag reels, but most of all, we needed to be alert and well back on the dock, because with no railing, it was a fast twenty feet to the water at low tide, and because the only things we were there to catch were stingrays and sharks.

Without actually seeing it, we usually knew what was on our line. If a shark hit, it would go in all directions and try to wrap the line around a piling. If a stingray hit, it would take off for the middle of the bay in a straight-ahead power thrust, and when it had all of the line, we had to make sure we were secure on the dock so we could begin the long process of give and take, which we optimistically referred to as "reeling it in."

The sharks and rays were too heavy to bring up twenty feet to where we stood so they had to be coaxed along the outside of the long dock to the shore in order to be landed. We always did the best we could to land each one, but it was tricky. The shark could usually find a way to bite the line, break the leader or circle a piling, making it necessary to cut the line, while he pulled loose and headed back home to sea. And the stingrays, with their Olympic quality butter-fly stroke, would often overpower our small arms and strain the line until suddenly we would feel nothing but the tide. Then it was time to take a deep breath, feel the wind, look at the water and the clouds, then add new line, leader, and hook and very carefully reach into the coffee can to select another mudworm.

In Fairhaven, even the worms were treacherous. They had black pinchers on the front. If they sunk into your finger with their notorious worm poison, the head would have to be cut off and the pinchers removed with pliers. Then your hand would have to be doused in alcohol, and you would have to start biting and sucking your own finger and spitting out the contaminated blood. And never drop one inside your overalls, even on a dare. I don't know if that was all true, because I never saw anyone get pinched. The natural tendency was to be wide-eyed and coordinated around mudworms.

I remember this one Saturday. We are there on the high dock. Several of us. The boats are out for the day. We have the dock to ourselves. We are standing near the outermost end. Five lines in the water. Two are Bill Loon's. One is mine. One is Bill Loon's younger sister, Mary Ann, who hates to fish and never comes because she never catches anything good. But her girlfriend, Sherry, has to go somewhere today, so she comes anyway. The fifth line belongs to Junior Malstrom who is Bill Loon's best friend. There are some onlookers. The group varies, but normally it includes some boys from North Fairhaven, which was sometimes called Finn Town, and a couple of younger Indian kids who are allowed to come and watch if they behave themselves, which they seem to do amazingly well considering Junior Malstrom is setting a bad example by jumping and cavorting around the dock a little more than usual. Finally Bill Loon tells him to sit down. But Junior reminds everyone that it's his uncle's dock and he can do what he wants. So Bill Loon, who is the same age and twice as big, tells him to sit down or he will throw Junior into the water and tell his uncle much later after the sharks have invited him home for dinner and an octopus family is using his bones for toothpicks.

So Junior Malstrom sits down.

And then Bill Loon's sister has to go to the bathroom, but there is no bathroom on Humboldt Bay that we know about. This is fine, if you are a boy. You can just go off the dock, next to a piling, holding your pole close. We all know that trick. But if you're a girl, it's a whole different card game according to Junior Malstrom who claims to know more about girls than most scientists. Time and again he informed us that there was no foolproof way for a girl to fish and pee from a dock at the same time. Too many things could go wrong. To hear his descriptions, I was sure he had seen it tried a lot of different ways. I don't know what dock he was on, but I was pretty sure it wasn't this one. Bill Loon called it Junior's dream dock.

Today Junior is silent on the subject and Bill Loon watches three poles while his worried-looking sister skip-hops off the dock and into the lupines and walks back two minutes later, smiling, with freckles dancing, ready to fish again.

She takes her line and tells everyone she will go back to the house in a while and make sandwiches, if we think we might be hungry later. Later? We tell her to go ahead right now, but Bill Loon looks straight at the sun and says it's only about 9:20 and not time for lunch. So we try to relax and fish.

Junior Malstrom catches a perch and tries to shake it off his hook. It's an embarrassment. And I get two crabs, which is worse. But then Bill Loon gets a medium size mud shark so we get our lines out of the water right away so as not to get tangled and watch as he expertly gets him nearer the dock and then works him around the outside and finally pulls him onto the soft sand of the shore. It's the first catch of the day.

Old Duck Fred pays thirty cents for mud sharks and fifty cents for stingrays. He feeds them to his ducks and geese, he says. A movie costs us twenty cents. The ferry to Eureka is five cents each way. A shark apiece will get us there and back. Two sharks means popcorn and a candy bar. Any more than that and we are into funny books.

It's about ten o'clock. We walk out on the dock and put our lines in the water again. It's quiet for a while so Junior Malstrom starts reciting dirty poems, which he always does to pass the time, and Bill Loon tells him to shut up, because his sister's there. But Mary Ann says it's okay. We laugh as Junior starts right up again. It's obvious she never heard them or she wouldn't say okay so Bill repeats it's not okay and Junior says he doesn't remember any more anyway. And we laugh some more because he is lying. And another crab gets my bait.

Then Mary Ann says, "I've got something," and she looks like she'd be happy no matter what it was. She stands up and shows us the bend in her pole. "See," and she smiles. It kind of reminds me of family fishing in Oregon.

"Open the star drag a little," her brother tells her. "Just so you get in the habit."

"I don't care if it's just a crab," she says. "I'll make crab salad sandwiches!"

I still remember exactly what I am doing, when I hear her say those words, "crab salad sandwiches."

I am looking up at the clean, blue sky. The morning fog has gone by then, not the gradual way it disappears in other towns, but blown about a hundred miles down the coast somewhere. I realize that I am right in the middle of the few jewel precious minutes of sunny, no wind weather we get each year, a time when the name "Fairhaven" no longer seems like the punch line to some long forgotten sailor's joke. Fairhaven: a spit in the wind; short on manners, but long on huckleberry grit; on the ground and in the air.

My daydream is cut short by Mary Ann's loud, hellish wail that shoots a spray of panic over the end of the dock. And time, as

I know it, simply disappears for the rest of the day, creating a deep memory inside, undisturbed and fairy tale perfect.

The first thing I remember was Mary Ann, Bill Loon's sister, who made great sandwiches and hated to fish, running sideways across Junior's uncle's dock, trying to hold onto her fishing pole and stay on her feet at the same time. When she reached the end, where the Jack Salmon II was usually tied, she tried to grab a loose rope that wound around a piling, but as she reached for it, the pole jerked and she spun in a half circle. She lost her balance and fell backwards off the dock, still holding the pole. She clawed at the rope and her fingers squeezed a spot above a knot and somehow, she held on, to everything.

Unable to even adjust her grip, she was hanging by an arm, facing the dock with one leg straight out, barely touching timber, and the other one dangling twenty feet above the water. One hand had the rope and piling and the other one gripped the fishing pole like it was the Holy Grail.

Bill Loon reached her first. His big hands gripped her ankle. We all came running close behind, but no one else could figure what to do next. Bill Loon could. He started right away to talk her up.

"You'll be okay. Drop the pole. Grab the rope with both hands," he said in an almost too quiet voice, as though something too loud might shatter the piling like fine crystal. "Do it without thinking. Right now. Then we can pull you up."

No one moved or took a breath. We waited for Mary Ann to drop the pole. But she wouldn't drop it.

"Sis, drop the pole!" Bill Loon said.

"I can't," she said, and her dancing freckles froze as she stared at us. She was more of a real fisherman than any of us thought possible. But, after all, she was Bill Loon's sister. Maybe it was passed along in the family bones.

"Take it, Bill. I can hold on until you take it. I will. I promise."

"Drop it before you go off!" Bill Loon shouted.

"Help me catch it. I never catch anything good. I want to catch this one," she said.

"Go! Mary Ann!" Junior Malstrom yelled to the seagulls as he leaped into the air. "We'll help you!" I didn't know what to do. Bill Loon whistled, and we all jumped to his side. So many hands grabbed her ankle, we were clear to her knee. As I watched him stand and stretch, I realized that Bill Loon had a body that was designed for some sport that hadn't been invented yet. He reached over and around the piling, grabbed onto something I couldn't see and swung forward, suddenly leaping right onto the top of it, spread eagle, piling to belly button. With one hand he managed to reach down to where Mary Ann was hanging and grasp the pole exactly in the middle so it balanced perfectly as she released it to him. But he was in trouble right away. Trying to get leverage with one foot to get back to the dock, he was almost pulled into the water when the pole started twisting like taffy. He reached with his other hand and opened the star drag. The pole stopped bending, but the cutty hunk line began ripping through the tightened fist of his bare hand.

Even I could feel it burning into his flesh. There was blood already. He pulled himself to one side of the piling and leaped, awkwardly, but accurately back to the dock and splinters went into his back as he hit wood. He scrambled to his feet and tried to take control of the wild pole.

Mary Ann had two hands gripping the rope now, so we all kept grabbing further until we had her jacket and found that with enough slow tugging and shifting of our weight, we could get her closer until we finally rolled her right up and onto the dock. She jumped up faster than a sand crab and followed her brother cross the dock as he ran sideways.

Bill Loon stayed far from the edge of the dock. For a moment he stood completely motionless. Maybe he was trying to figure what it was on the line. Not even his wide-set eyes moved. Maybe he thought the fish was gone. It happened that way sometimes. Mary Ann came up next to him.

"You're not mad at me, are you?"

Still he didn't move. That meant he wasn't mad. It took an awful lot to get Bill Loon mad and it was nearly impossible before noon. He started reeling in very slowly with his bleeding right hand. He was dripping on the dock.

"Is he gone?" Mary Ann asked. We waited.

"No," Bill Loon said. "Bring something for my hand. The reel's getting sticky." And then like a reverse bolt of lightning had suddenly shot through the dock end of the pole, down the other end went, nearly bending it in two, pointing, straight at the water below and nearly causing Bill Loon to bend in after it. But Bill Loon was fourteen and he was big and he could fish. I don't mean which hook, what bait and where to stand. I mean he could really fish. Like Lash LaRue or Mighty Marvel.

Leaning back, he slackened the tension on the drag and wrapped his leg around a piling, just in case, and he started winding the reel again. Mary Ann brought a piece of T-shirt and covered the inside of his palm where the blood was coming out.

What was it? It went toward the middle of the bay like a ray, but it went in random patterns like a shark. No one knew. Finally Junior Malstrom broke the tension with a couple of theories. First he thought it was an electric barracuda that had been in an A-bomb blast. Nobody even paid attention to that comment. That was probably the movie we'd see if we could ever catch enough fish to go this afternoon. Then he said the only other thing it could be was a saltwater crocodile. Evidently that made more sense. At least everyone looked over at him, which he interpreted as a standing ovation. Smiling, he began to elaborate.

Bill Loon never took his eyes off the water. That meant only one thing to me. Whatever was on the hook would not be going home tonight.

Every once in a while, he let his sister hold the pole, when the line wasn't burning friction sparks into the air or the rod wasn't nearly breaking in two or the reel wasn't whining out of control. He wanted her to get the experience, I guess. I was getting plenty from right where I was.

After alternating portions of strain, sweat, wonder, worry and enough layers of Junior's commentary to bury all of us standing up, the mysterious thing we had been waiting for suddenly spiraled close enough to the surface for all of us to see from the dock.

Mary Ann shrieked louder than before. She was right next to me. It was so unexpected, I screamed too. I think I even went into the air an inch or so without bending my legs. I had never done that before. And my hat blew into the bay before I could catch it.

"Cut the line!" Junior cried. "It will tear the dock apart! My uncle will kill us!"

It was a nine-and-a-half-foot tiger shark and in spite of its long ordeal, it wasn't tired. It was chewing the piling directly under us. The dock was shaking.

"It's okay, Bill. You can cut him. He's too big for you. Let's catch something else," Mary Ann said.

His concentration was so strong, I don't think he heard her. "You and me, Sis. We're bringing this one in," he said.

Everyone shut up, closed their eyes and tried to imagine they were somewhere else. Anywhere. Junior Malstrom tried to turn Catholic. He started crossing his chest with his fingers. He wasn't joking around either. He said he heard it was okay with the Pope as long as you really meant it. He was probably lying, but I didn't care. I did a few myself.

The tiger shark was throwing his body against the pilings and barnacles flew in all directions. He flipped his tail into the line and twice it looked like Bill Loon was going to buy the bay for his sister. I looked down at the churning water, up at the sky, and every once in a while I crossed myself again, just in case I didn't get a chance for last rites.

It worked. It was a miracle. Bill Loon didn't go in the drink and the dock didn't collapse. We finally got the tiger shark around the dock and on the sand, I say we, because by this time, anyone who stayed on the dock, felt like they had cheated death and were part of the deal.

As it thrashed on the wet shore, none of us could believe how big the monster was. It opened its jaw and flipped its tail and hit Poley, one of the Indian kids, right in the back and sent him face first into the sand. He got up and walked right back to it and said "Grrr" like he was a bear, but he wasn't hurt and he wasn't mad. He was just surprised. Bill Loon motioned to us to keep back. The big tiger shark was still dangerous. He pointed where there was a bullet and some buckshot in him.

"Somebody knows who this guy is," Bill Loon said. "I didn't even know there were tiger sharks around here. This one is rare."

We were so tired we just sank quietly in the sand around the beast and waited while it died. Afterward, when it didn't move anymore, Poley, the Indian boy, leaned over close to it.

"I say you were a good fish," he said.

It sounded funny the way he said it, but it was true. Bill Loon stood and took off his hat. So did Junior. So did Mary Ann. Everyone did, but me. My hat was in the bay. I rubbed my hair and halfheartedly crossed myself again. Together, we rolled the shark over on its back while Junior who had been jumping and holding himself ran to the nearest log.

Bill Loon took his huge hunting knife and sliced the animal open all the way down the middle in order to clean him. That's the way Old Duck Fred wanted his fish. On the last swipe, we jumped back because ten or so little sharks flew out and flipped around in the sand. We thought the big tiger had eaten them for breakfast. Out of courtesy to Mary Ann and respect for the present direction of the wind, Junior was facing away, softly singing yes, yes, yes to himself. He turned his head when he heard the commotion and suddenly shouted, "That tiger shark is a cannibal!" not realizing he had turned too far. Everyone caught quick glimpse of something that was better left unseen. It happened so fast, to be truthful, I don't know what I saw, but it was connected to Junior Malstrom and I swear a river ran through it.

He finished his private moment with his back to us. But that didn't stop him from shouting over his shoulder, "Cannibal! Cannibal!"

"No! No!" Mary Ann yelled. "He's wrong. These are babies. She's a mother. This is her family." She quickly began to carry the first of the newborn sharks to the water. We lined up like a bucket brigade and began passing each of the remaining ones to her while she stood knee deep in the rolling waves and eased each one of them for the very first time into their real world of salt water. At first, they went in circles, showing off their shiny new tiger fins in a little shark show. Then two bumped into each other, turned upside down and died. When the rest of them saw that, they decided the show was over and disappeared.

We were tired and out of the mood for any more fishing. Except for Bill Loon with his mud shark and whatever Old Duck Fred would give him for the monster shark, none of us had caught anything to sell so we wouldn't be able to take the ferry to Eureka and go to the movies.

I looked at the huge tiger shark right side up again. It looked like it was still alive. I had an idea. What if we covered it, propped its mouth open, and wheeled it house to house and charged twenty-five cents if anyone wanted to see it. Maybe we could go to the movies after all. Bill Loon smiled slowly and over to one side. He sensed there was something basically wrong with the idea. He looked at Junior, then his sister, then the rest of us.

"We can put it on a couple of wagons," I said.

"It can't hurt anything," Junior said. "What can go wrong?"

Bill Loon nodded and we cheered. "But don't get your hopes up. This is a fishing town. People may not want to pay to see a fish," he said.

It took all of us to lift and roll the big tiger shark onto the wagons. We covered everything except the wheels with an old green tarp and started down the road, taking turns pushing, pulling and walking alongside like an honor guard.

At the very first house we knocked at, the woman yelled out the window, "Don't bury that bastard here!" She had been drinking and thought it was a funeral for an army deserter. She said she knew there was a body under there and if she had a phone, she would call the police. Junior Malstrom smiled and asked her if she would come to the door for just a second so we could explain quietly what we were doing. He was very comfortable talking with adults, even if they were upset, so he was our spokesman. The woman saw his smile and then realized how young we were, so she opened the door. He thanked her for hearing us out and then told her that if she tried to tell the police, there would be two bodies under the tarp. Before she had a chance to jump away, he whispered something to her. I don't know what he was saying, but her eyes got smaller and smaller. Then she said, "Okay," and threw us twenty-five cents to keep it covered and go away.

A few people paid, some weren't home, and then one man, a big lumber worker, said he didn't have twenty-five cents, but he wouldn't mind taking a look for free. He said there were no tiger sharks around here anyway. Then he laughed and started coming out the door. He was a renowned bully, but Junior didn't mind. He was comfortable talking to bullies. He stood in front of him and said, "You don't really think there is a tiger shark under there do you? You think it's a trick to get your money."

"That's exactly what I think, Short Stuff," he said and laughed again like it was Jack and the Beanstalk and Junior had his goose.

"Okay. You can look for free," Junior said. "Why, thank you," the man said.

"Don't thank us yet," Junior said. "Because there's one condition. If it is a tiger shark like we say and you don't pay, we get to put a curse on your house. Okay?"

"Okay," the man said. "This house is pretty much cursed anyway." And he laughed again.

"You just think it's cursed," Junior said. "Wait 'til you hear our curse. If you don't pay by thirty seconds after we show you, and I'll be counting, at the next high tide in a rainstorm, fifteen of these air breathing man-eaters are going to come crashing through your windows while you and your dog are asleep and have their way with both of you from all sides!"

We jerked the tarp off. The man shot backwards into the house and slammed the door. Junior motioned for us to wait while he counted very loud, "One thousand eight, one thousand nine . . ."

The man opened the door just a crack. "Do you have change for a dollar?" he asked.

"No," Junior Malstrom said with a big smile. "One thousand twenty-eight . . ." The door closed again and a dollar bill floated to the ground in front of us.

"Lumberjacks don't know nothin' about ocean fish," Junior said as we started off for the next house.

We weren't having much luck, then one lady seemed absolutely delighted that we were there on her doorstep. She even told Junior he gave a nice presentation about why we had come. Afterward we realized that for some reason, she completely missed the word "shark." She was so thrilled that we kids were participating in what she called "a neighborhood enrichment project" together, instead of roaming the sand dunes, looking for trouble and becoming juvenile delinquents. She said she was on a blue ribbon committee to improve children, but maybe she could learn some things from us.

"You never know," Junior said, smiling like Mona Lisa.

She said she was more than glad to give us twenty-five cents to see our little traveling educational project, as she called it. She waited. Junior held out his palm. "Oh, of course," she said. "Here's a quarter. Now what is it you really have under there?"

"You got wax in your ears, lady? We got exactly what we said. A giant tiger shark!" And the tarp came off.

She could scream louder than Mary Ann.

"That's a nasty trick. You could stop somebody's circulation with that thing! Shame! Shame! How did you catch that? Not on somebody's dock I hope. Do your parents know about this?"

Junior Malstrom loved it. He was comfortable talking to club women.

"Of course, they do, ma'am. There were ten adults supervising the whole time. It was sponsored by the Sea Scouts. Everyone had to wear two life jackets just to get on the dock. The Coast Guard, even the Mayor was there."

"What Mayor? We don't even have a mayor," she said.

"Not anymore we don't. He blew right off the dock. Everybody did. Except us. We are the only survivors."

"You are a little fibber. Soap's not good enough for your mouth. Shame! Shame! I want my twenty-five cents back," she said. "Right now."

"I wish I could do that, but my hands are tied," Junior said, holding both wrists together. "We are a no-profit enriching group. Libraries, museums, art places, movies, funny books."

"You are nothing but a bunch of outlaw hooligans, charging money for heart attacks. Your parents are going to hear from my committee. So are the PTA and the sheriff."

After that encounter, Bill Loon said to leave the tarp off. He decided it wasn't good morals to charge people money to see a dead animal once we had enough for us to go to the movies. Besides he said he was getting a headache listening to Junior Malstrom talk to the neighbors. Giving them malarkey, scaring them half to death and then taking their money.

"This is how lynch mobs get started," he told us.

Junior disagreed. He said that in order to get lynch mobs going, you need a horse or a woman that doesn't belong to you. Bill told him not to count on it.

It worked out a lot better when we left it uncovered. People were friendlier when they could see it coming. They acted a lot more normal. Just about everyone smiled and wanted to know which one of us had actually caught it. Without hesitating, Bill Loon said it was Mary Ann's catch, but her freckles started dancing and she turned red and said Bill helped her more than just a lot. But he said he talked her through a couple of tough spots. That was all. Did we shoot it for her? No, that was done some time ago. It was her catch all the way. Line catch. No guns. Look close, see? Old wounds. So by that afternoon, and in the days that followed, it was generally known and accepted that Mary Ann Loon had caught the biggest shark from a line on a dock that anyone could remember on Humboldt Bay. Later on, she got her picture in the paper and the cannery, whose workers had been constantly terrorized by it and had tried to shoot it, were giving her a hundred dollar reward until they found out she had put ten more of them back in the bay.

For some reason, Junior Malstrom was angry at Bill Loon for letting Mary Ann take all the credit. Bill said that's the way he wanted it. He said it was a present to her. Just like a birthday or Christmas, only instead of giving her something he bought or made, he gave her something that happened. "You can't give something that happened to somebody else. It's against the laws of nature," Junior said.

"There will be years and years and plenty of chances for me to catch all the fish I want," Bill said. "It may not be that way for Mary Ann."

"Not the crazy ass way she fishes, it won't," Junior said.

The three of us were walking back to the Loon house to celebrate. Junior and I were invited to dinner. The sun was setting over the sand dunes. How could it be getting dark? I was thinking it was still morning when I was looking at the peaceful sky, and heard "Crab salad sandwiches!" Time is so funny.

I realize Junior is still arguing and Bill is tired. But Junior keeps it up and Bill decides to grab Junior's wool shirt, lift him up and start screaming in his eyes. "I want you to see this picture, Junior. Mary Ann is willing to go in the bay so she can catch a good fish. And she gets lucky. Now, while I am gutting it and you are pissing over your shoulder yelling 'Cannibal,' Mary Ann is putting more baby tiger sharks back in the bay than most people are going to see in their whole life. That's why she deserves it. And if you ever mention it again, you are going to be stuffed and mounted right here on the front of my house, next to my dad's moose you broke the antler off of. That way I can talk to you every day without you yapping about who caught the tiger shark. Mary Ann caught the tiger shark!" Bill puts him down. "Okay?" Bill asks in a quieter voice.

"It's not okay!" Junior is madder than a half-boiled lobster and almost as red. He swings at Bill Loon, but Bill jumps back and I almost get it in the face. Their words and actions are all mixed up, like seeing a book right in front of me, blowing in the wind, without any words to read. Junior is on Bill Loon's back hitting his ears. Bill spins around to throw Junior off and his engineer boots almost take off my head. I'm too small for these guys. They are fourteen years old. I realize that words seem to come to me sometimes out of books I've never read. That's why I'm mixed up. Now I'm seeing what seems like a book and nobody even wrote it.

I jump away to find some tall grass on solid ground where I can feel safe until it's over. But in Fairhaven, grass is scarce and the only solid ground is sand. And sand is the oldest servant to the wind. It has been sifted and scattered side-angle through so many centuries of constant whim, all that's left is the shifting shadow of something once solid. I dig my heels into the softness of the servant and wait. No wonder I don't feel safe in Fairhaven most of the time. The three elements of life around here: wind, sand and water, make little room for fire. Even a flame as small as mine. I see they are laughing and shaking hands at last. I come out of the lupines. They want to know if I ran away because I got scared or if I went to take a pee. I don't answer.

They laugh and tell me they're sorry. They say I almost got clobbered a couple of times. Probably almost killed, Junior has to add, nodding his head way up and down. I know they don't play with eleven-year-olds. They are so old they probably don't even call it play anymore. I don't even know what they do call it. I know they don't call it work. Yet it seems to be their work. I tell them that I'm kind of tired after everything, today. Maybe I better come to dinner some other time. They tell me no, no, no. They want me, Mary Ann wants me, his mother wants me, his dad, everybody. They do? I don't understand. I'm glad everybody wants me to eat, but I don't understand.

"You must be one of those guys who are so smart, they are stupid," Junior says. "I read about them."

"Where? In Classics Illustrated?" Bill Loon says and hits his knee. "You came up with the idea to take the shark around. That's why. It's turned out to be the biggest thing around here in a couple of months. Somebody came by. They want to put Mary Ann's picture in the paper."

"Besides, you're funny and you don't eat much," Junior says and we all laugh.

I'm glad everything is quiet and stupid again. No more fights tonight, I hope. As we are sitting on the front porch of the Loon house, smells of steaming food are coming out of the screen door. Candles are burning brightly on the dining table. Fire has been allowed to show itself in Fairhaven at last. I feel safe. Bill's sister and mother are making dinner and laughing, freckles of two generations dancing all over the kitchen.

American Horse Racing or
Larry Larsen's One-Eyed Horse

I RODE STRAWBERRY UP to the starting line, my hand cupped toward her ear, trying to stir her wild part with animal words that would probably sound to anyone but me and Tarzan like mumble mush.

"Kreeg-ah! Bundolo!"

Ignoring me and the commotion around us, she turned her neck sideways and fixed her good eye on the long, gray airstrip in front of us, not knowing what was about to happen or how far it was to the sand drop-off at the end. She limbered her front legs, an old habit, and then nodded her head a few times like she suddenly remembered being young again. Maybe the Tarzan talk worked. When she finally turned her head back to look at me, I was still trying to find my safe spot, which was the one place I could lean into the wind at full speed without running the risk of being denatured. I found it and settled a hair left and just a little behind the old western saddle horn. It was Palm Sunday and I had a week of vacation to look forward to if I lived through this race.

Three days before, Bill Loon had said "Strawberry's missing the one thing that horses need for real racing."

"A real jockey?" I had asked.

"Two eyes," he had quickly answered back.

If he was right, and Bill Loon usually was, I could be in trouble with this race. "Let's face it. With Strawberry here, one light is out," Jake Fowler, class clown of the fifth grade, had said one day. I thought that she made up for that problem, because she seemed to trust my eyes in the several sprints we had done, even the ones that didn't leave us enough room to stop. She didn't mind two of the times it happened, because we ran right into Humboldt Bay and she got to cool off fast.

Bill Loon told me if she sensed I was the set of horse eyes she needed to judge distances, she would be more than likely to think in horse thoughts:

"Oh what the hay, I got legs. I'm born to run. Let the skipper navigate. If the Great-Horse-God wanted me to have two eyes, he wouldn't have poked one of them out."

Bill Loon thought horses were a lot smarter than they let on. I told him that if they were that smart, they'd open horse colleges. They'd be riding us.

He lifted each of her hooves and made sure her shoes were sized and solid. He did a little scraping, a little tapping and every once in a while, Strawberry would scoot in a circle. Bill Loon patiently followed her around until the ticklish job was done.

"Shoes ship shape, General," he reported like we were in the horse marines or something.

General Custer, that's what Junior Malstrom called me sometimes because he thought I was always galloping Strawberry into some disaster. Today he might be right.

Below, some other kids from Rolph School were laughing and trying to fool each other with the old reach-around-and-tap-your-other-shoulder trick. Sherry Ferston was standing in front of them with her big, natural smile that seemed to be all over the place. Mary Ann was beside her. Sometimes they held hands. A lot of girls did that because the wind on the spit was sometimes vicious and liked to blow everyone around a lot.

Sherry, almost thirteen, was a clean, deep breath of ocean air and excitement to me. She had black shiny hair swirling on her shoulders in slow motion and perfect dusky skin. Mole, mole, who's got the mole? Not Sherry. She was seamless. Her skirt was flashing up and around her tan legs like she was a loom for the flags of freedom. I saw she was still smiling, shaking her head at me. Her deep brown eyes were pouring right into mine over the top of her outgrown, pink eyeglasses. I thought I knew exactly what she was thinking, but I could never be sure. Girls think differently. Finally she shouted at me, laughing.

"It's a good thing you weren't born a girl. You can't say no to nothing." It was a joke we had. Supposedly Warren Harding's father said that to him when he found out he was running for president.

I looked away from her as Junior Malstrom began to make an announcement through a megaphone he had stolen from the high school gymnasium.

"Is there anyone who hasn't paid yet?"

No one moved.

"Good. Now this race is a prepaid, non-sanctioned, independent sporting event."

"What the hell does that mean?" One of the adults from the more than fifty or so spectators called out.

"It means that if the police come, you are on your own. The sporting event is officially over at that point. We suggest that you leave immediately in different directions. Preferably toward the sand dunes," Junior said. "When you get to the ocean, go to the right and follow the coast a ways and then come back a little north of town. You'll be fine. And good luck."

"Is this thing legal?" a man called from the crowd.

"Technically, yes. There are no laws on the books, because this type of racing has never been done before. I call it true American horse racing. There may be a law in the future if things don't go well today. This is a very unique and dangerous event. Does anyone want their money back? This is your last chance."

No one moved.

"Okay, we'll be starting in a few minutes." Junior Malstrom put the megaphone down.

Two ragtail sentries, obviously paid partially in bubble gum, were waving all clear from the sand dune that separated the highway from the small airstrip. The two-lane road was seldom used and ran out to the U.S. Coast Guard base at the end of the peninsula.

Mesmerized by Junior Malstrom's announcement, the thrill-seekers were huddled together in the wind that blew across the airstrip. It was normally posted with a NO TRESPASSING sign, but it had been covered by a large towel and secured with thumb tacks specifically for the event. A hundred circling seagulls screeched the location of the group from high above, but no one paid any attention.

Cars and bicycles were parked every which way. There were mostly pre-war sedans and a surplus jeep belonging to some of the bachelors who worked at Mutual Plywood. The two pickups belonged to some Indian families. The bikes and soapbox racers belonged to the spit kids, which was the name outsiders some-times called us. It essentially meant half-wild, outdoor toilet types. Big deal. Our family had an outdoor toilet for the time being. You get used to it.

Bill Loon and Junior Malstrom were already in junior high and they rode the bus seventeen miles around the bay each day, while most of us were in Rolph Elementary School, which had been standing in the sand by the bay for as long as anyone knew. It faced the fishing boats and the real town on the other side, Eureka, California.

Today there were a ton of town kids. The visiting team, so to speak. They were all Junior's invited guests. He said he only invited the best. The top drawer of the high school shop majors from Eureka and Arcata. They all arrived in hot rod coupes, road-sters, and stripped-down motorcycles. They were flanked by their pluck-browed girlfriends. The custom was to seal their love by zipping them into their car club jackets for safekeeping. The girls looked like disaster victims in sleeping bags. The boys, all in jeans and white T-shirts with rolled up sleeves, had goose bumps.

Junior Malstrom had cooked up this kettle of horse flesh and steel stew during one of the long bus rides to school, according to Bill Loon. All it seemed to take for Junior to get the duck's butt haircut set hopping onto some hot coals was a few dares and a quick look at his eye-popping roll of ten-dollar bills, which I knew for a fact had one bill and the rest newspaper. I was there when he carefully cut the newspaper. Junior was sort of an artist, but you couldn't really get him to draw anything unless there was a payoff.

Two weeks before Junior told me if I would ride Larry Larsen's horse in a race, he would give me a long list of really good stuff he had. It was a Pandora's hope chest for delinquents. When I said no, he just added more items and kept talking. He had so much steam in his pitch that he finally clouded my mind just the way The Shadow did to the crooks on the radio. After a while I couldn't think clearly. I was being dragged through the weeds of crime toward the bitter fruit.

"There's not even another horse on the spit. What am I going to race?" I protested.

"A car," Junior said. "You are going to race a car."

"A car? It's Larry's horse. Let Larry ride in your race!" I shouted when I came out of the trance. "I don't want his mother hunting me down like a rat for the rest of my life if something goes wrong."

"What could go wrong?" Junior asked.

"The car could hit the horse, for one thing!" I shouted.

"Why would a car hit the horse if they are both going the same direction?" Junior asked.

"Because the car is going faster," I said.

"Look, Larry can't ride. He's afraid of his own shadow. You can ride fast. I heard your grandfather rode for the Pony Express. I've seen you ride Strawberry. You can make her move so she looks like a brand new horse. And don't worry about Larry's mother. I'll handle her. She's a pansy!"

"She's not a pansy!" I said. "She's a cobra."

"Doesn't matter. She'll never know. You have the Malstrom 100% personal guarantee. Top Secret. Just like the Normandy Invasion," he said.

I pulled my hand back from the handshake. "The Normandy Invasion! That's no secret!"

"Not now it isn't, but it was then. Afterward everyone involved was a hero. The secret was out, but they were heroes. You are going to be just like those soldiers. And you're the general! Riding your horse onto the field of battle!"

"Racing a horse on the beach right in the middle of the Normandy Invasion? Everyone would remember me all right. Front page of *Look*. 'The Morons of World War II!'"

"Calm down, Custer," Junior said.

"Don't call me that," I said. "It makes it worse."

"Okay, General. Whoa. Calm down. Shh. Listen. Everyone is going to be sworn to secrecy. And, look here," he said.

He pointed to his old, customized Schwinn bike. He had done a lot of stuff to it like remove fenders, put on long horn handlebars and added stuff that made no sense like a hand siren, a horn, and a few playing cards clothes-pinned against the spokes, but it was still the best-looking bike on the spit.

"What?" I said. "I get the bike? Mine?"

He nodded.

"Do I have to win to get it?" I said. He was winning me over.

He shrugged a maybe.

"I'm going against a car, for criminy Dutch!"

"Okay. Okay. Maybe you don't have to win. It depends. You have to do your best and not chicken out."

"I won't chicken out," I said.

"I know you won't," Junior said. "If you do your best, you got the bike and all the rest of the stuff too."

"Really?"

"Really," he said.

We shook hands.

It didn't happen very often, but I could actually feel my balls getting sweaty. With a morphodite horserace like this was, most kids, even if they were sworn to secrecy with threats of torture and death, couldn't hold it in. It would be the only way to get their bodies to stop shaking. With no phones on the peninsula, no TV, a fresh clean scandal was the best entertainment around. A good story about a juvenile outing gone bad could blow through the peninsula faster than an afternoon squall and eventually right into the ear of my father who would be compelled to take me out behind the mushroom shed and level the arm of justice across my rear end.

@

He had an uncle, my father did. Uncle George. One time in 1913 he said that he actually had a foot race with an Arabian stallion in a small town in Minnesota. And won. I got to thinking that maybe me racing a horse against a car wasn't that different. It was part of my heritage. Maybe it was the true meaning of American horse racing. Like evolution. I thought about that for a while as I sat in the saddle waiting.

@

Suddenly Strawberry. Whoa! She didn't like something in the air. Gasoline. Her nostrils swelled. She raised her head high, lifted her front legs in the air like Gene Autry's horse, Champion, and dumped me right off the back.

"Caught me by surprise!" What could I say. The crowd laughed and pointed, moved back and a few kept laughing even after I led Strawberry around in a circle a bit and then bounced back up in the saddle. It was funny, but it wasn't that funny.

The Ford was finally running, but the flimsy hood was still up so I knew they didn't think it was running right. It was hard to tell what a ride like that was supposed to sound like. You'd have to be around it a while on a quiet day. I suspected there wasn't a part on it that some junkyard dog hadn't peed on first. One guy was holding the hood so it wouldn't come down and fall on the head of another guy who was poking and staring at the carburetor while he was shouting back and forth with the driver who I couldn't even see because of the custom narrow windows. The driver raced the engine every once in a while to make it get smooth, but it was like beating a kid to make him stop crying.

"Easy. Sh. Sh. Sh. Easy," I said to Strawberry as we walked in a circle while she eyed the noisy monster with distrust.

"Hey are we going to do this or not?" Junior Malstrom's voice was back on the megaphone yelling toward the group around the car.

He was ready to pedal his Schwinn (the one I might soon own) to the far end of the air strip and flag the winner at the finish line. He was getting too old for the bike. It was time for a car for Junior, even though he was only fourteen and not old enough to drive legally. This race was part of a plan he had to get his car, and he was going to see that everything went right. He was going to win the Ford (he only wanted the LaSalle transmission out of it), but most important, he said to everyone, "I want nobody to get killed today if it can be helped!" No wonder people were paying to watch. I would probably pay myself if I wasn't one of the ones getting killed.

His bike, with its newly applied half deck of cards held on by clothespins up and down the front fork and rear frame, made it hard to even push, let alone ride. That one bike sounded like a motorcycle gang cruising into a small town.

The car suddenly died and wouldn't start again.

"Pull the caps off the lake pipes," the driver's voice yelled to the two under the hood. "That's the only way we are going to smooth this out enough to run the race!"

"What the hell are you trying to prove with your stupid tune-up? You got a flathead Ford that barely runs. You're going against Larry Larsen's one-eyed horse with a not even twelve-year-old jockey who three days ago couldn't even spell horse. This ain't Indianapolis. Get started and get up to the line!"

"Pipe down, Malstrom. Like I said, I'm going to win this race without ever going out of second gear. You watch me. Now shut your trap, or I'll come over there and shorten that pair of jeans of yours so you can see the rest of your ass!"

The driver probably didn't know it, but Junior liked it when tough guys badgered him. Particularly older ones. And bigger ones. It kind of got his juice churning, especially if there was anybody watching. And today there were plenty watching. It may have been the biggest audience Junior ever had. At first he hung his head like he was kind of scared so the guys and the car coat girls around the Ford all laughed. Then, like a red herring at the last supper, Junior waved his checkered flag over his head.

"Watch this folks," he said to the Fairhaveners and shuffled off to Buffalo toward the Ford camp like a tap dancer. He leaped onto the low roof and started tapping out a soft shoe routine. He was humming, singing and tapping his fingers on his stomach.

". . . I've even got the horses clopping bop down the avenue. Folks love the rhythm. The slam bammin rhythm. You get a lot of kick outa the blacksmith blues. Be doubie doubie doo."

By the time he finished, Junior Malstrom had crunched another two inches into the already chopped top of the Frankenford.

The driver's swear words carried out the little side window and across the dunes. The car almost started, then the clutch slipped and the car jumped forward, knocked Junior off the top, and the engine died again. All three of the Ford crew and a couple flying packs of Luckies went after him, but Junior's timing was flawless. He was already halfway up a sand dune, picking his teeth with a long strand of dune grass. The crew returned to their car and the crowd clapped at the sideshow. Even if there was no race, nobody would have asked for their money back by then.

❦

Three days earlier Junior told us he wanted this car for one thing: the transmission. It was out of a 1938 LaSalle, long winding and solid. It would be the beginning of his handmade dream car. The rest of the car was crap and scrap as far as he was concerned. That's why he was betting that a horse could beat it. It was the pink slip against Junior's flashy wad of money. That was the bet. He told them he would pay them $200 of it if the car won the race. I knew there wasn't $200 to even start with. There was only $10. And that was if the ten-dollar bill was real.

"I am ready to get behind the wheel and drive like a man," he said. "Like all the men before me."

"Drive like a maniac, you mean. Like all the maniacs before you," Bill Loon said. "Your brother drove his first car two years before he ever used his brakes. He went to sell it and found out it didn't have any. Drove two blocks right past the buyer's house and hit a tree."

"That was an accident," Junior said.

"You are right." Bill Loon said. "That's what they call it when a car hits a tree."

❦

Junior yelled to the crew from atop the grassy dune.

"They can hear you all the way to Samoa with the noise that piece of junk makes! That's if you get it started again. It practically scared the horse to death. What the hell kind of race track courtesy is this, anyway? It's supposed to be fair and square. The best car you can come up with and the only horse we can find. And you can't even get to the starting line!"

The crowd laughed. Junior slid down the grassy dune on his back. The crew all gave him the finger as he raced past them. He bowed to the crowd, put down two hats in front of them. Side bets.

"This one is for the horse. Even money. This one is for the car. Twenty to one." Junior called out.

"In other words I put in one dollar in this hat and the car wins, I get twenty dollars?" a man said.

"That's right," Junior said.

"And if I put a dollar in this other hat and the horse wins, what happens?" another man asked.

"You get your dollar back," Junior said.

A few people were scratching their heads, muttering, "That's not a very good bet."

"Who's the bank?" the man asked.

"I am," Junior said and showed him the phony roll of ten-dollar bills. "Larry, would you watch the hats and take the money?"

People started putting their money in the car hat.

After two tries, the hood slammed down and stayed shut. The crew guys took screwdrivers and undid the end of the lake pipes that ran just underneath the rocker panels along the bottom of the car. We waited for it to start.

"In the south they would have made that car into a still," Bill Loon said to me.

I knew he was trying to make small talk to keep me calm as he held Strawberry's halter. I looked more closely at the car. Mostly it was a 1939 Ford Tudor Sedan. No big deal. There were probably thousands of them. But this one had been lowered front and back, nosed and decked with a chopped roof, which had now been danced on and dented to the point you had to squint to see in. Nothing had as much privacy as that car. Not even an outside toilet.

When they started the Ford again, it was ten times louder than the plywood plant. And soon it was obvious the springs were shot as well. It drove up to the starting line like a coffee can somebody was shooting at.

Strawberry's good eye started watering. She was really hopping now. Bill Loon used all his weight to hold her in place. The noise was causing people to hold their ears.

"You better not hurt my horse!" Larry Larsen yelled up at me. That's all I needed.

"How could anyone hurt your horse?" Junior said, putting his arm around Larry's shoulder and leading him back to the crowd. "Your horse is over there and that little putt-putt car is way over there. I'll be watching to see that nothing happens and flag the winner. Win or lose, you can ride home to mom a full five dollars richer! And you can tell her 'Hi mom. See I'm famous. Larry's Famous Quarter Horses.' Oh and watch these hats for me, Larry."

"There is only one hat," Larry said.

"Oh, the one with the bets for the horse must have blown away. There wasn't anything in it," someone from the crowd said.

"Nobody bet on my horse?" Larry cried out. "That means she is going to die!"

Junior Malstrom pulled him aside so the crowd couldn't hear.

"It's better for us," he said to Larry. "That way when the horse wins, they lose. Get it?"

"No," Larry said.

"Then I better keep the money, Larry. Everybody remember how much they bet?" Junior asked as he stuffed the bills and coins in his jeans.

"Yes," everyone said.

"Okay. I'm trusting you all," he said. "You are on your honor."

"Still you better not kill my horse!" Larry yelled again.

"Do you know how hard it is to kill a horse?" Junior screamed at Larry Larsen.

"No," Larry said.

"Well, it's pretty diddly darned hard. It's almost impossible unless you are really stupid! And I don't see anyone here who looks stupid, do you?"

"Yeah, lots of them!" Larry yelled back.

The kids started hitting Larry.

"Okay. Okay. Nobody looks stupid," Larry said.

"Say it. Say what I just said about killing a horse!" Junior screamed at Larry.

"It's diddle doodle hard to kill a horse unless you are really stupid," Larry said.

With that sentence from Larry, Junior jumped on his bike and weaved down the runway waving the checkered flag as he went. It was a long way down to the finish line and the drop-off.

@

As I watched him, I thought about years earlier when I rode a horse for the first time. It was the Lazy J Ranch near the Oregon coast. We knew the owner, McPeak, and so we stayed there sometimes on vacation. He lifted me up on top of Old Cross, a dapple gelding whose real name had been Double Cross when he was younger and wilder. He had two prominent Xs on his rump. It was a bad branding, McPeak said, that caused keloids that stayed red for years. I was four then and my brother, behind me in the saddle was two. He was facing backwards, I don't remember why now, but it was all right with him. At least we both fit in the saddle. I remember McPeak tightened the cinch around the belly, and pointed us in a direction toward the circular corral and handed me the leather. My first reins.

"Neck reins, like this. Not like this. Don't pull. Reins against the neck. Try it. Good. Pull to stop but not too long or he will start to walk backwards. You'll figure it out. Best way. You're born to ride or you're not. You're starting young. That's a good sign. You're not afraid. That's another."

I watched as my mother, father and McPeak walked away from us up to the lodge.

"Are they safe on that horse? He is so big," my mother said.

"I'd put a baby on that horse," McPeak said.

When they were gone I said "Giddyap Cross."

"He didn't say go giddyap," my brother said in his baby voice.

"Everybody says giddyap," I said.

"Giddyap, Cwoss," my brother whispered.

Old Cross almost brushed him off the saddle with his big tail as we started moving around the corral. But before I could stop him, he found an opening in the fence and began a slow, jarring trot down a steep hill, came to a large log barn and stopped against it. We waited, but he didn't move. He was leaning flat against the log wall. I couldn't get him to budge. Finally I threw my brother off into the grass. He started crying until I jumped off after him. He stopped after a while. We both looked up at Cross's head. His eye didn't move. Maybe he was dead.

We walked back up to the lodge and found my mother and dad at the bar. They were drinking highballs with McPeak and playing punchboards.

"Back already?" McPeak asked.

"Are you all right?" my mother wanted to know.

"Sure," I said.

"We got a big kweston," my brother said.

The grownups laughed, because his baby voice was so funny.

"What?" McPeak asked. "What do you boys want to know?"

My brother looked at me. "Can a horse die standing up?" I asked for him.

"No," McPeak said. "If he died, he would fall over."

"Can't die standing up?" I repeated.

"No, he'd have to be leaning against something," McPeak said.

"Like a bawn?" my brother asked. There was a long pause.

"What happened boys?"

"We just wode your horse to death," my brother said. "Can we get another one?"

☙

"You want me to pull the saddle off fast and you can go bareback?" Bill Loon was talking to me. "I can fix a rope around him tight for you. Won't take a second. Could be a lot lighter. A lot faster."

It could be a lot quieter around here too, I thought. My God that car was loud.

"No, leave it," I said. "We are almost ready to go anyway."

"You better not kill my horse!" Larry Larsen yelled up at me again when he saw that Junior was far away. "I'm not kidding. If you hurt my horse, my mother will kill me, but she will kill you first."

"Do you want to ride her?" I screamed at him.

Larry backed away. I caught a glimpse of Sherry again. She wasn't smiling anymore. She actually looked a little worried as she and Mary Ann held onto each other. The crowd was laughing at the way Larry was jumping around.

"Don't laugh! She'll kill the rest of you too!" Larry screamed at them.

☙

I remembered three months before when Larry's mother decided to get him the horse. I was outside on the front porch of the school, because I had gotten excused early when I finished my spelling and geography and was bothering everybody. I had to wait for school to be over for my half-hour piano lesson. The familiar green Larsen Chevy paddled across the hog fuel chipped parking area in front of the school throwing plywood chips behind it until it stopped. It was just before 3 p.m. Ida Mae Larsen looked straight ahead through the windshield with a fresh Camel hanging from her dance hall mouth. Her elbows rested on the plain, worn steering wheel while she scanned the scene, obscured only by the clouds of her own smoke. Soon the kids started running past me out the front door of the school and down the steps. Ida Mae Larsen looked like a rustler's wife waiting to snatch one of the little doggies for veal cutlets when they ran past her to the afternoon freedom of the open lupine fields. She watched as the thirty kids emerged from the front door.

Some kids ran right to her car and announced that Larry had been set back a grade that day from the fourth grade to the third grade.

"It's no big deal," someone said. "He only has to move over one row."

Her eyes blinked. A flurry of Camel ash flew around the front seat. She rolled out of the car like a sack of live salmon.

"Why didn't I know about this first?" she screamed.

She spit the Camel out of her mouth as she climbed the steps, releasing a spray of embers that glowed brightly, even in the afternoon sun. There was loud yelling inside the building.

I waited in one corner of the front porch for her to come out and leave so I could go back into school to start my piano lesson. Everyone else was watching from the safety of the lupine bushes that surrounded the school.

Finally the door flew open and out she came, dragging Larry by one hand.

"We lost the battle Larry, but we didn't lose the war!" she cried out in the afternoon wind.

"What war? It looks like a soap opera to me," Jake Fowler called out from the lupines.

"I see your damned little eyes out there. None of you is half the student my Larry is. None of you will ever know what it is to be a fine sportsman. A boy's boy that will someday grow up to be a man's man, because he has the guts to pull himself up by his own bootstraps."

"He has to," Jake called back. "He doesn't know how to tie his shoes yet!"

"You little ingrates! Within a week, mark my words. You will be over at Larry's house, begging to be his friend, because Larry is going to get his own horse!"

Everyone started laughing and heading home. I shot back through the front door of the school before Mrs. Larsen could see me and into the piano room. I gave the round stool an upward spin until it was the right height and sat down, looking at the yellowing keys of that kindly old piano. For a moment I saw Ida Mae Larsen's teeth, but quickly put it out of my mind. Miss Nickols came in the room looking red.

"Hives," she said. "Show me that you practiced this week. Another big shock might make them go away."

She stayed red all during my lesson and I got a gold star with a minus after it again.

⦿

Two weeks later, a covered horse trailer slowly drove though Fairhaven like it was the Pied Piper looking for the Rose Parade.

Just about every kid on the spit was following it by the time it turned in at the long, scruffy driveway of the Larsens. There were words on the side of it that were too faded to read.

"I hope whatever is in there is younger than the trailer," Jake Fowler said. We ran to watch as Larry and his mother came out of the house, and the wrangler went around the trailer, opening the rear gates.

"Let me have that halter," Mrs. Larsen said, overpowering the wrangler. She quickly began trying to walk the horse backwards out of the trailer with a few quick snaps of the leather lead. The ramp was narrow and the horse, whose head was bobbing, missed the ramp with her right rear leg about halfway down and started falling toward us. Sherry Ferston grabbed my jean jacket just in time, and we spun sideways. We cracked branches together through a huge lupine and hit the ground, just missing being crushed by the frantic horse, who quickly stumbled back to her feet.

"That is not a very stable horse," Sherry whispered to me as we got up from the broken lupine branches. "It's not a very good horse for Larry."

"I don't think it's a very good horse for anybody if it can't stand up," I said.

"She can stand up okay," Sherry said. "And I'll bet there was a time when she would run like the world was coming to an end. Look at those rear legs and that neck. She's a quarter horse, I think. But something is wrong. I can't tell. Maybe she's crazy. Oh my god. Look at her head. On the right side. Wall eye. Larry Larsen has a one-eyed horse."

"Okay, who wants to ride Larry's new horse first?" Mrs. Larsen yelled out.

"Do we look like Kamikaze pilots?" Jake Fowler said. "Oops, sorry Mrs. Larsen. I didn't mean it! I'll wash my mouth out with lye as soon as I get home. I meant that we think 'cause it's Larry's new horse, he should get to ride it first."

"Yes, let Larry get on it first," everyone cried out.

"My Larry, you look great in your new white outfit honey, just face the hat the other way. My Larry is already twice the horse-man any of you could ever hope to be. So who is going to be first?"

"I'll go," Sherry said.

Cheers of relief came from everyone.

"Don't any of you brave boys want to go first?" Ida Mae shouted.

Silence.

"Ladies first," Sherry said, holding out her hand for the reins.

"Watch that skirt in this wind, Sherry, or you're gonna look like Lady Godiva with a bad umbrella," Jake shouted.

I could tell she had ridden before. She maybe went to a good summer camp and learned, because up until that day there wasn't anything to ride on the peninsula that even looked like a horse.

"What's her name?" Sherry asked

"Strawberry Roe. She's a race horse. Larry will be training her," Ida Mae said.

Sherry mounted quickly and rode the horse up the long san-dy driveway, turned and came back, then she turned and took Strawberry to a little canter, up and back, up and back. When she reined up in front of Larry and got off, the horse was almost se-rene. Sherry was pushing her little kid glasses back up on her nose, and I was getting stirred up inside a little, watching her, which had nothing to do with anything I could understand or talk about right then. It had to do with Sherry. She was so shiny. Even with stupid glasses, she had to be the best-looking girl on the west coast. She was better looking than the girls at the rodeo and even movie stars. Elizabeth Taylor would give her a run for the money, but Rosemary Clooney and Joan Crawford sure wouldn't.

"Can I go next?" I asked.

"I thought you spent your time taking piano lessons. You need riding lessons too?" Ida Mae said.

"I don't need lessons," I said. "I used to ride up in Oregon."

"Yah, we used to ride up in Oregon," my brother said, suddenly appearing. "One time we rode a horse to death."

"Where did he come from?" Ida Mae whirled around.

"He was right there by the lupines," I said.

"In the lupines, you mean. He wasn't *by* the lupines! He scared the bejesus out of me. Where the hell's my cigarette now?"

"Me and my brother rode him down a hill into a log wall and killed him dead. It wasn't our fault. They said it was suicide," my brother said.

"Well, I don't want you two death riders on Larry's new horse at the same time, ever. You understand me? We're not ghost riders in the sky around here." Ida Mae's cigarette was safely back between her curled lips.

Her teeth did look like that old piano at school.

I looked down at everyone as I got into the saddle. It felt good. Bobby Benson of the B Bar B; Gene Autry and the Melody Ranch; Monte Hale down the gun-smoking trail to the Dallas Kid's last stand; Red Ryder and Little Beaver; Kid Colt Outlaw. Take your pick. Up on a horse, you could be anybody. "Giddy up." She started forward at a walk.

I kept seeing Sherry out of the corner of my eye. She watched me with her head cocked, dress snapping ripples in the side wind, adjusting her glasses on her nose. I really liked her. Everybody liked her. But what I was feeling was different. Something was going on inside me. It bothered me. Was I thinking about trying some cowboy stunt on this one-eyed horse? Was it because of Sherry? No. I put the thought out of my head. Once up and back was plenty for right now. I thought Strawberry was okay. She understood I was up here in the saddle and turned when I pulled on the reins, but she had a lumpy trot and, on the right side, she couldn't see for oat crap, but she didn't fall over and that was enough for me.

"I bet they snatched her out of the waiting chute at the glue factory," Jake Fowler said. "Or we would be using her for salt and flour maps."

"Mrs. Larsen said she is a registered quarter horse," Sherry said. "Maybe it's true."

"George Washington was a registered general too. But after a while you die," Jake said.

"She still could be a quarter horse. Bred for racing in the quarter mile."

"She probably is. A quarter of a horse with half the eyes and a third of the teeth," Jake said.

"I've got to get home," Sherry said. "You just don't like horses, Jake, that's all."

Jake said he wanted to stay around to see how many more times the horse would fall over before somebody actually died, so Sherry and I started walking down the road toward my house.

"Mrs. Larsen is so funny. You'd think Strawberry and Larry were getting ready for the Kentucky Derby," Sherry said.

"If that horse was that good, Roy Rogers would have bought him," my brother said, coming out of the lupines.

"Where did he come from?" Sherry said jumping, then turning around and looking at him.

"Same place we all do, I guess," I said.

Sherry hit me on the shoulder and her silly little glasses fell off in the sand. We bumped heads trying to pick them up at the same time.

"That was fun," I said, rubbing my head. I knew the minute I said it that it sounded stupid, but it was too late.

"You want me to drop them again?" she laughed.

I knew my brother had been walking along with us behind a row of lupines. He did it a lot. He liked to break twigs and point them at things.

"Back home in Corvallis, the neighbors were always mad at him for bending their bushes. That's why he likes it here. There are thousands of lupines to snap and no one even notices," I said.

"Is he an Indian?"

"No, I don't think so. He's just my brother," I said.

"Maybe I am and maybe I'm not," my brother said, turning and disappearing into the lupines.

The next few months were nuts. Horse nuts. Larry Larsen, Rolph School's newest third grader, was right in the middle of it as a full-fledged mock celebrity. First everybody wanted to transfer to the third grade so they could get a horse. Then poetry started popping up for extra credit by kids who couldn't spell any better than Larry. "Leary Leary, Kwite Contary, how does your spelling go?" Stupid stuff like that. Miss Nickols said regular poems would get you extra credit for language arts. Poems about Larry would get you cleaning erasers after school. In spite of all her efforts, he was "Strawberry Larry, The Texas Ranger who couldn't spell Texas." They said his wonder horse helped him cheat in arithmetic by tapping her hoof outside the classroom window.

There was a brand new safety rule Jake Fowler made up. Before crossing the street, look both ways so you won't get run over by a horse. He came up with that when Larry came riding up one day, bouncing and holding onto the saddle horn.

"Hand me those long leather things so I can get her to stop," Larry was saying.

On Halloween, he went trick-or-treating as the headless horseman, and Strawberry walked through the front door of somebody's house before he could stop her.

On Thanksgiving, the school decided to have a "Pilgrims of Plymouth Rock Pageant" starring Strawberry who showed up pulling a wagon full of Pilgrims and a live turkey with Larry in the driver's seat. When the Pilgrims saluted the group of Indians with their cap pistols, Strawberry took off for the bay and dumped the whole crew in the sand next to the water. The turkey escaped into the lupines.

For Christmas, Strawberry came to school with red poster paint on her nose and a skinny Santa Claus on her back.

"Hey look," someone yelled, "It's Rudolph the Red-Nosed Reindeer and Larry's dad dressed like a skinny Santa Claus!"

"Good luck trying to get your presents on time this year," Jake said.

After a time, Larry got to just walking Strawberry to school. It was too hard to get her to stop, once he got there, he told everyone. He would walk her up to the steps and tie her to railing like he was the Marshall of Fairhaven or something. He was supposed to exercise her every day, and his mother thought he was, but he didn't want to, so he let me ride her in the afternoon instead. He liked to ride his bike better anyway, he said. I gave him a little of my Christmas candy each day in exchange. I was to never tell his mother, which was fine with me. I didn't like to talk to her anyway. Her teeth always reminded me I wasn't doing that good in my piano lessons.

Once on Strawberry, I felt at home in a make-believe world. I rode and rode. I pretended to go lots of places and do lots of things as different famous cowboys. Then I started riding by Sherry's place. Her father's redwood shingle mill was way out in back of their house. I'd go out there first, and her dad would laugh and ask if I needed any shingles. Then he'd say, "Why don't you see if Sherry's around. I bet she'd like to go horseback riding."

"Oh, okay. Maybe I will. If you think it would be okay."

Sherry and I would take turns riding and then we would ride at the same time with her in the back mostly. I don't know what she was thinking, but I was thinking it was still the Old West. The neighbors could see that we were riding around a lot, so we got kidded. Sherry was pretty tough for a girl. I might get mad and end up in a fight with somebody who kept on and on about having a girlfriend, but Sherry would walk right up and knock their block off. So the teasing was kept in tow.

While we were riding, we talked about a lot of stuff I never thought much about before. We got so we would ask each other questions about things we didn't know. I wanted to know why girls wore dresses. She wanted to know why boys tried to see under their dresses. I told her because they wanted to see what day it was. One peek and oh, it's Thursday already. Test tomorrow. Thank-you, Ma'am. She said I had a good sense of humor for my age.

Sometimes we would leave the horse tied to an electric pole or just leave the reins hanging while she rested. Strawberry waited patiently while we would go look for arrowheads under and around the lupines. We made tunnels under the bushes as we searched. We would lay back and rest every once in a while and Sherry would run her hand along my crew cut and ask why I had my hair so short. I told her I didn't know. They just cut it that way. She asked me to tell her something I *did* know. I said I did know that my hair would never look as good as hers when it blew in the wind if I lived to be an old man. She rolled her eyes in her head. "Twelve years old?" she said. "When are you going to be thirteen?" Truth be told, I hadn't quite turned twelve.

One Saturday morning when we weren't fishing, one of the Indian uncles from the Low Eagle family appeared in the morning fog. Kind of like my brother often did. Where the sudden presence makes you jump.

"Can I try your horse? I'd like to show you something," he said.

"Sure," we said.

"Watch," he said. He took the reins out of my hands and rolled onto Strawberry and within seconds turned her into a one-horse stampede. He galloped way down the hog fuel road to the bay and back.

"Old. Very fast," he said when he returned. "Sleeper. You could win money with this horse. Looks beat, but run good for cyclops."

We watched, amazed. He had been some kind of horse trainer as far as we could understand from his short sentences. He showed me what to do to make her "outrun the wind, my friend."

"We don't need to go that fast," Sherry said.

"Unless we are after bank robbers," I said.

"We don't have a bank."

"Ride like that. Now and then. She will learn to trust you. Pretty soon she will be good shape. Be happy. Racing quarter horse. You know that? Fastest animal in quarter mile," he said.

I told him I thought that a cheetah was the fastest animal. He told us yes, a cheetah was faster than a horse sometimes, but nobody could stay on a cheetah for a whole quarter mile so it didn't count. Soon he was gone in the morning fog. *Maybe my brother was an Indian.*

After that, I started riding Strawberry the way the Indian did and I think that's the reason I got targeted for the horse racing scheme of Junior Malstrom's. That's also when I got to know Sherry a lot better than I ever expected. She was like a guy in a lot of ways, but there was definitely a difference. The way she looked, of course, and then there were the funny books. I had most of the current westerns. Or so I thought. She told me about a funny book series called Saddle Romances. She had ten of them. I looked at the covers, but I wouldn't read them.

"Why don't you?" she asked. "It could give you some ideas."

"About what? Sewing calico? Baking prairie pie? Bottle-feeding homeless buffalo calves?"

"You never know," she said. "You might read about some things you might like. About life." She was almost a year older than me, but I knew what she was talking about. At the end of some of the stories, a cowboy would hug the ranch girl and her bonnet would fall off. No thanks.

"Did you hear the joke about the farmer's daughter?" she asked, holding my waist as we galloped along toward the bay one day.

"There are a lot of them," I said. "But I don't want to hear any when Strawberry is going about a hundred miles an hour!"

"The one about the bedpost?" she yelled in my ear.

"I heard it," I said. "Don't tell it."

"Embarrassed?" she yelled again.

"No, but we are going so fast, if I laugh or look around, Strawberry might go right into the bay! Whoa, Strawberry. It's the bay already. She's not slowing down Sherry!"

Strawberry took a leaping dive right into the water and soon she was up to her belly, and we were sopping wet from all the splashing.

"Sorry," I said. "I couldn't get her to stop. I don't think she saw the water."

"It's okay," Sherry said. "But I'm soaked. Let's get to your lupine fort. We can dry our clothes on the branches above."

I suddenly got worried and I guess it showed in my face.

"You can leave your underpants on," she said.

As a starting pistol, Bill Loon's .22 revolver did not work for beans. With the wind, the babbling Ford, the seagulls, the crowd cheering, and Strawberry snorting around like a jackrabbit in jail, I didn't even hear it. Nobody could. He stuffed the gun back in his long army sack and pulled out a single shot .410 his father had given him. He put in a shell, locked, and fired into the air. Seagull feathers flew in all directions, but no birds dropped and everyone certainly heard the shotgun, even the driver inside the Ford who should have been deaf by then.

Bill Loon replaced the shell from the smoking shotgun, looked down the strip to check Junior at the finish line, then nodded once for Mark, once for Set and then fired the shotgun into the air. This time two seagulls fell to the ground. That was illegal, I'm sure, but so was just about everything else right then.

I snapped the reins on both sides of her neck as fast as I could. It was time to travel, and Strawberry's clock must've told her to kiss tomorrow goodbye. She dug into the blacktop runway surface like a finger-painting four-year-old and almost left me sprawled at the starting line. I don't know where she learned it, but she could accelerate and she didn't let up. God in the garden, she was fast. Hold on to your tulips. Easter was coming early.

The Ford roared, popped, and laid rubber until I could hear it squealing and fishtailing out of control behind us. The driver saved the spinout with a snap into second, and the rear wheels finally caught pavement. The clapping V-8 sounded like it was going over the top of us. But the sound only made Strawberry run faster. All the driver had to do was shift into high gear and blow past us. But he didn't. The LaSalle transmission just kept the engine winding higher and higher. I was clear over Strawberry's neck when the Ford came up right on our tail. She started veering to the side. I tried to pull her back toward the finish line, but she seemed determined to escape the engine noise anyway she could.

Then suddenly she caught a glimpse of Junior's frantic yelling and pointing with the flag. She shifted direction back the other way and started going toward the Ford like we were in an aerial dog fight. The Ford didn't let up and would have used our blood for the red carpet to victory if the driver had just shifted into third, but he didn't. He wanted to be able to say he won this race without ever leaving second gear, like he had promised Junior. But then Pow! Just like in the funny papers. With a little caption above the car. Pow! And the engine headed for heaven. Well, not exactly heaven. Too much fire for heaven. The driver tried to save the day by releasing the gearbox into neutral and freewheeling across the line, but the loose hood popped up and billows of smoke made it impossible for him. Flames shot from the engine. The driver's door flew open and he leaped out onto the runway just as flames covered the car. Someone said that as he rolled, the blacktop ripped his T-shirt and pulled the engineer boots and wool socks right off his feet. The car spun in an arc and came to rest harmlessly at the side of a sand dune.

Strawberry and I shot past the finish line where Junior Malstrom was jumping and yelling and waving his flag. "The winner and champion!" he called, but nobody could hear him but me.

"Whoa. Whoa. Race over. Strawberry! Oh jeez!"

I pulled hard on the reins and tried to turn her, because we were out of runway and came upon the steep drop-off. But I was too late. I stayed with her until we were high in the air, then I had to jump clear. Pegasus, the flying horse and Dum Dum the Dutchman.

I opened my eyes and saw Junior Malstrom looking upside down at me from the top edge of the runway. I was nearly buried in sand. I stood up. I was okay. Pretty soon Strawberry got to her feet and worked her way toward me in the steep sliding sand. To this day I have no idea why she was coming toward me. After that ride, I would have tried to get as far away from me as I could. Covered with sand, maybe I looked like her mother. Miraculously, Strawberry was not injured.

We climbed back up to the runway and when our heads appeared over the blacktop surface, there were stares and silence, then shouting and cheers like I never heard before. The group ran to meet us about halfway back to where we had started. We passed the Ford, still smoldering. Junior was leading the way back on his bike, and I was behind him, back up on Strawberry. Sidesaddle. I was too dazed to walk. I remembered that statue with the Indian and the horse. *The End of the Trail*.

The group was wild with yelling and cheers. It must have been some race. It seemed like I was only half conscious since coming out of the sand so I had no idea. I remember that Sherry Ferston was biting her lower lip when I jumped down right in front of her. I saw her eyes. She had tears in them. I had sand in mine. She grabbed my shoulders. She was looking me up and down and squeezing me to make sure I was still alive. When I looked at her, I knew I was very much alive. I guess that's what it means to have a girlfriend.

"You stupid sonofabitch, Malstrom! Here's your pink slip and there's your car! The fire should be out in an hour or so." The driver was carrying his boots in one hand and his socks in the other.

"Thank-you," Junior said. "The transmission's still good, I bet. Even if the engine is gone. You almost made it, you know. Better luck next time."

"This Fairhaven is a spook show," the driver said, while his girlfriend struggled to put his socks and boots back on. "Ow, take it easy," he said. "Let's get out of here."

The motorcycles and cars from the mainland started up and one by one went out through the entrance, each with its own salute of noise and spirit, and onto the little highway that headed north toward Samoa, Arcata, and eventually Eureka.

◉

Strawberry was lathered and pretty sandy. *Who wasn't?* I was still dopey as I led her in a circle to cool her down. Larry Larsen ran up and almost knocked me over grabbing the reins.

"You almost killed my horse," he said. "I'm telling my mother too."

"Your horse will be fine," Sherry said. "You should be happy to have such a great horse."

"Get away from me," Larry said. "You're a girl. My mother says you are, well, never mind. Don't even talk to me and don't talk to my horse either. Either one of you. Ever!"

Junior Malstrom kissed his signed pink slip. He told me I could pick up his Bombay Schwinn (that's what he called it) at his house later, as promised, and he initialed and slipped Larry the five-dollar bill like he said he would. Larry stuffed it in his jeans pocket without saying anything. Junior tried to split some of the booty with Bill Loon, for acting as groom and starter, but Bill said he was donating his time and the ammunition to the cause of American horse racing. And the book he had bought on how to shoe horses? Well, he would have eventually bought it anyway. He loosened the saddle, pulled it off to give Strawberry a breather, and put it on the sand next to the runway.

"Perfect race! Everybody did great! You were great too, Larry! Did he hear me?" Junior Malstrom was shaking hands with everyone. "Anyway, it's over and done and nothing could have been more perfect. Just enough excitement. Nobody killed, nobody caught. What did I tell you, Custer?" *For some reason I hated that name.*

Sherry Ferston faced me while the crowd moved around to be near Larry and the flying horse. They wanted to help brush the sand off Strawberry.

"Don't touch my horse," Larry told them.

"When she went off the end of the runway, I thought she would roll right over you," Sherry whispered to me.

"Almost did," I said. "It was my fault. Can't blame it on your farmer's daughter joke this time."

"She looked like a real race horse, little General. Just like in Kentucky. Come here. Your eyes! How can you see? You've got so much sand in them. We'll brush them off in a minute. Right now we are going to do the winner's circle."

She took her glasses off.

"Oh boy. Here it comes. Right out of Saddle Romances," I said.

"Shut up," she said and then she kissed me. I was probably redder than Strawberry if you could see through the sand. But nobody saw, because everyone was buzzing around Larry and his now famous flying quarter horse.

"He is such a little pea picker," she said. "But we should help him get her cleaned up anyway. It is his horse, after all, and he let us ride her all these months. It's the reason we got to know each other. You know what I mean. Oh no. Larry! Don't tie her to something that small. She could pull it and get tangled up!"

"Shut up, B-E-C-H!" Larry yelled back.

Larry had tied Strawberry to a long piece of driftwood while he went to get the saddle. He turned around telling everybody once again to stay away. He was mad, because Strawberry was wet with lather and sandy and he knew he had to get her cleaned up, but he didn't want anybody to help him. He picked up the saddle, spitting, swearing, and walking backwards, swinging it from side to side. When he spun around, he was too close and banged the saddle right into Strawberry's back legs. She spooked and ran a few feet, dragging the piece of driftwood behind her. She turned, trying to get it loose, and it tangled around her front leg. She twisted and leaped up trying to get out of the rope and driftwood, but she fell forward and rolled. She got up and tried to run again, limping a little this time. It was her front leg. It wasn't holding her anymore. She whinnied and ran in a circle, trying to shake loose the pain of what was now a broken leg. She fell again. This time when she got up and shook it, the leg was hanging only by tendons and skin.

With everyone screaming and yelling, I tried to walk to her, but she backed away. She didn't trust me anymore. I couldn't get the reins at first. Panting and winded, she finally let me touch her head.

"You've got to turn her head to the side and lay her down." It was Bill Loon.

I reached up and gripped the bridle. Strawberry lifted me clear off the ground, swinging me in all directions as I held on to her head. I twisted her nose up one way, her ears down the other way. She resisted so I held my feet off the ground and kept turning her head until she could no longer keep her balance and crashed sideways onto the ground. Everyone stood around while I held Strawberry's head down on the blacktop. Thank God, her good eye was up, but she was in pain.

Bill Loon spoke. "We can't save her. Her leg is completely torn up. If she was a million dollar pony, we couldn't save her."

"Well, she is a million dollar pony," Sherry said. "And we have got to."

"I know," Bill Loon said. "And we can't."

It seemed like forever that I held Strawberry's head down. Every so often she would kick her back legs, and then settle down. Some others were helping to keep her down until we could figure out what to do. Sherry brought a jacket to put under her head.

We wiped her down and waited. Larry had run off to his house to tell his mother. Bill Loon told us that we should just keep her quiet until Larry's parents got back and told us what they wanted to do. We should put her out of her misery right then, he said, but it wouldn't be right without the owner's okay. We waited. Strawberry was quiet after a while, but she was breathing more heavily as time went on. She was now covered with fresh lather. I talked to her. A lot of us did. It seemed to help, but I knew she was still in pain.

Finally, Larry returned with his parents.

"What happened here? Who is responsible for this?" Ida Mae asked.

"Larry tied the horse to a piece of driftwood and she got tangled and broke her leg," Bill Loon said. "It was an accident."

"It wasn't an accident. I heard there was a horse race here. Horse against car!" Ida Mae said.

"They raced my horse with a car and the car blew up and my horse broke her leg!" Larry shouted.

"This has nothing to do with any race. The event was already over. Larry got his horse back in perfect shape. Besides he gave me permission to use Strawberry anyway."

"No, I didn't!"

"My Larry doesn't lie," Ida Mae said.

"Mrs. Larsen. There is a five-dollar bill in his pocket," Junior Malstrom said.

"That's my five dollar bill," Larry said. "He didn't give it to me."

"It has my initials on it," Junior Malstrom said. "I am sorry about the horse, but Larry is the one who tied her to the driftwood. It was an accident and it was after the event. And besides I paid him."

"Paid him for what? To kill his horse?"

Bill Loon whistled with two fingers and scared the crap out of everybody. "We're holding Strawberry down right now, Mrs. Larsen and Mr. Larsen. She is in pain. We've been waiting for you. What do you want us to do? She should be put out of her misery," Bill Loon said very softly.

"Haven't you criminals done enough? And who was riding her anyway?"

I didn't want to hear that question.

"It's your decision. If you want to call a vet, we'll hold her down, but it may take a couple hours for one to get here." Once again it was Bill Loon.

Mr. Larsen finally spoke. "If her leg is broke, and it is, look at it. It's barely hanging on by skin. We can't wait for a vet. It wouldn't help anyway. Do you have a gun?"

"Yes," Bill Loon said. "I have a .22."

"Can you put her down? I'd appreciate it. We'll arrange to have her taken away tomorrow."

"If you kill her, you can pay to have her removed!" Ida Mae yelled.

"Come on, babe," Mr. Larsen said. "Let the boys handle it," and they got in their car and drove slowly out through the entrance. I could still hear Ida Mae's voice until they were out of sight.

Bill Loon got his .22 revolver out and wrapped the barrel with a red neckerchief. "I'll cover her eye," he said. "It will be better that way. Here, put the muzzle just behind her ear. Then fire. Twice."

"Me?" I asked.

"It should be you," Bill Loon said.

"Why?" I asked.

"You are the one she was closest to. You are the one she trusts. Her owners have left her. It's your horse now."

At first I wouldn't take the gun, but I looked at Sherry and then I looked back at Bill Loon. I figured there was some kind of unwritten code that everybody else seemed to know about. I didn't want to do it, but I took the gun. I tightened the red neckerchief around the barrel.

"She'll jump. It can't be helped. Everybody hold her down firm," Bill Loon said.

I couldn't believe I was doing this. I wasn't even supposed to shoot birds with my BB gun.

I said "Goodbye, Strawberry. It will be all right in a minute."

For you, maybe. Not for me.

I fired the revolver three times as fast as I could. The rear end of Strawberry flagged the air several times and twisted, but then she stopped. We all stood up. Straw pies came out the back and urine appeared in a pool around her hips. I handed the .22 back to Bill Loon handle first. The neckerchief had splashes of blood on it. I shook out my arms. We had held her on the ground for nearly a half hour. I ached all over. My face was wet and swollen.

"Are you okay?" Bill Loon asked.

I wasn't. I tried to answer, but I couldn't even talk.

"Come here, Baby," Sherry said.

"I'm not a baby," I tried to say, but it wouldn't come out. I turned and started walking away and then running. I wanted to get to the dunes.

"I'll get him," I heard Sherry say. "Stay here."

I ran until I stumbled on some low lupines and fell forward. Sherry fell on top of me and held me down.

"You've had a real big day, little General. Time to take it easy."

Her arms and legs were around me. I could smell her body, which was good, but I could smell mine even more and it was like horse. Her heart was thumping right over my back and her breath was all over the back of my neck. It was like I was back in the race only it was me being ridden. I tried to get away, but I only got a few feet with her still on top. Then I rolled over to one side suddenly, and I was on top of her. When I did, her legs tightened around my lower back, and she held on to my jacket collar. Our faces were nearly touching. I couldn't pull away. I thought she said please stop. I thought I was hurting her, because her legs seemed to be kicking my back. That's when the feeling started happening and stuff changed fast. We knew we should try to untangle, so we wrestled a little, but I pinned her arms in the sand above her head. I realized that she had slowed her movements and was looking right into my eyes, letting me hold her down. It was the worst time and best feeling I ever had in my life. For several seconds, I didn't even know or care where I was. She pushed her hips off the sand and back down again. When I caught my breath and looked, I saw her eyes were closed, she was breathing through her mouth, like we were still running. I wasn't shaking anymore.

"Better?" she asked.

Her eyes flashed fresh like mirrors. Even with sweat and her head full of sand, Sherry Ferston was so good looking, she could probably stop a hurricane with a smile. I would have told her, but I still couldn't talk. *I didn't know you could do it with somebody like that.* She brushed some sand from my lips.

"That was a real surprise, wasn't it?" she grinned and even laughed right out loud and kept pinching my cheek. "Felt that before?" I nodded. "With somebody else?" I shook my head no. "Me neither."

We walked the sand dunes until it was dark, holding hands. When it started to rain, we watched the drops wash each other's face.

"You want a saddle story ending?" she asked.

I nodded as we held hands facing each other. When we were finished, I pulled my lips away.

"If I had a bonnet, you would have knocked it right off, General."

We separated and I started off for home.

"Rest," she said. "Especially rest your voice. It needs quiet right now. You don't have to say anything until you get it back. Remember that."

☺

I arrived home wet, smelly and ready for last rites. I couldn't think. I couldn't talk. Ida Mae Larsen was there, raving and hitting her knuckles on our low ceiling when I walked in.

"Aha!" she pointed right at me. The Eureka police were there, too. They had been out to the peninsula for a while asking questions, but they were having a hard time finding anyone to ask. At last they had me, but Ida Mae wanted them to arrest me and then go talk to everyone.

"We're not going door to door tonight. Period, Mrs. Larsen. There may have been some hooliganism going on at the airport today, but your boy was involved too, so what do you want us to do? Arrest everybody in Fairhaven?" It was the big officer talking.

"Grill this little sand rat to start with. Look at that face. Pure guilt. He rode my Larry's horse to death and he knows it. You know it, don't you?"

Where was Junior Malstrom's guarantee now? I thought. *Where was Junior? Would I ever get the bike now?* My father was looking sternly at me, shaking his head. I would soon be out behind the mushroom shed, unless they decided to lynch me for being a horse thief instead. I didn't know which would be worse at this point. I couldn't even talk enough to plead innocent. I just pointed at my throat and made a little sound like a dying goat.

"So it's our animal and we have to pay to have it removed? That's just adding insult to injury! I called about a truck. It has to be a dump truck with a winch. Did you know that? Do you know how much that costs? I want this culprit, right here, the one they call Custer, and his parents to agree to repay every penny to us. If Larry gets another horse, that's up to us. But the dead horse, the one we used to call Strawberry, has to be hauled away. And this hard-riding little pucker head. Sorry, that's a little strong, he should pay the freight. He and his brother, that one, over there, they already rode one horse to death up near Bend, Oregon, you know." Ida Mae was in an unbelievable rant.

"I didn't see anything," my little brother said. Nobody paid any attention to him.

"Would you agree to that? Pay at least part of the cartage?" The little officer asked my father.

My father looked long and hard at me and didn't speak for a long time. Finally he asked me simply, "Custard or Custer? They name you after the pudding or the massacre?"

I opened my mouth this time and pointed way down my throat. *Don't they understand? I can't talk. Oh, for God's sake, bring me a coffin.*

"So, were you racing the horse?" my father asked.

I fell into a chair. I was out of everything. Not even any water for tears.

My brother spoke up again. "I didn't see anything. And if I didn't see it, I don't think it could happen." But once again nobody paid any attention to him.

"If that isn't guilt, I don't know what is," Ida Mae said, pointing right at me.

"Anything else ma'am?" the big officer said. "There is not much else we can do tonight. You'll have to come in and file a complaint."

"Yes there is something else. I want Junior Malstrom hunted down and prosticuted!" she said. "He was the ring leader that turned all these younger patsies into gamblers and horse thieves and killers. He is hiding out somewhere right now, like a coward, laughing and planning his next caper, leaving his little henchmen to squirm."

As the officers were about to leave, there was a quick little knock. "Yoo hoo." It sounded like a housewife coming to borrow sugar. My mother opened the door.

"Is Mrs. Larsen here? I've been looking all over the peninsula for her," Junior Malstrom said.

"Get him," Ida Mae screamed. "Before he gets away!"

"Can I come in? It's wet out here. Thank you. Good evening, officers. I saw your car out there. I thought you might be able to help me find her. Nasty night to have to come all the way out here to the spit, huh? Oh there you are Mrs. Larsen, crouched in the corner."

"I'm not crouched. I'm standing here. You better check and see if your car is still there, officers," she said with a smirk.

"I'd like to help if I can. Maybe I can clear up some things," Junior offered.

"So you're Junior Malstrom. I expected a much older, larger boy," the big officer said.

"I had polio," Junior said.

"No he didn't!" Ida Mae screamed.

"Were you racing this woman's horse?" the little officer asked.

"You mean her boy's horse. Larry Larsen's horse. The old mare, Strawberry?" Junior said pretending to have a lot of trouble getting the water off his face.

"Here's a towel," my mother said.

"Don't give him your towel!" Ida Mae said. "He doesn't deserve it."

"It's my towel," my mother said. "I'll do whatever I want with it."

"Okay. Okay. Please, ladies. We don't have all night. Just wipe yourself, Mr. Malstrom, and tell us. Did you race the Larsen horse?" the big officer asked.

"No," Junior said.

"He's lying," Ida Mae said.

"Did you have someone else race the horse for you? Did you arrange to have the horse race against a car out at the airport? And did the horse break a leg during the event and have to be shot? Any of those things?" the big officer asked.

"No," Junior said. "We were out for a Palm Sunday picnic with some kids from my school. We were about to go over to the ocean and collect some driftwood and Japanese floats for our science projects, when Larry came by on his runaway horse. He had lost the reins and couldn't get her to stop. While we were helping him, somebody thought it would be funny if Larry's horse, which is supposed to have won the Kentucky Derby, according to Mrs. Larsen—"

"I never said that," Ida Mae snapped back.

"Somebody said the horse could run faster than Bob Cooley's old Ford. But it was just a joke. You see, officers, even though she is supposedly a quarter horse, she can't race. She won't run."

"She won't now. She's dead." Ida Mae said.

"Please, Mrs. Larsen," the little officer said. "Let the boy tell his story. Why won't she run, son?"

"I'm sure Mrs. Larsen told you this but Strawberry only has one eye, officer. She is just a half-blind old mare. She doesn't have the bio-popular vision that horses with both eyes have, so she can't gauge distances at all. She doesn't know if she is almost next to something or if it's a hundred feet away. So, naturally, she is afraid to run. Can't blame her, poor thing. She is wandering around in a sad, flat world with no depth or judgment. That's probably how she came to live at the Larsens'."

"It is not!" Ida Mae said.

"Mrs. Larsen, I want you to know that Larry told us she wouldn't run. He couldn't get her to run at all. And by golly, he was right. The little guy knew his horse, sure enough. He let two or three of us ride her. Nobody could get her to go very fast. Your Larry is quite a horseman, Mrs. Larsen. I've heard you say that yourself and you are right. You can be proud of him."

"Oh, shut up," Ida Mae said.

"I'm sorry you are feeling bad, but I'm only telling the truth. Anyway, Bill Loon, our friend, he's studying to be a Norseman, I think. Anyway he told us why. It was because of the eye. I guess it was the way she was when the Larsens got her, where was it again, from McCoy's Rendering in Arcata? Maybe she didn't know Strawberry had only one eye. Maybe they didn't tell her. Maybe they didn't know. There would be no reason for them to check. You don't need two-eyed horses for what they were using them for. Glue. Anyway because of it, she wouldn't run. She might prance a little, but she would slow right down if there was any-thing around. There's no way you could race her. She would have to trust the rider so much that she would forget about the fact she couldn't see that well. And there is no rider like that around here."

"Very colorful, Mr. Malstrom," the big officer said. "Then what happened?"

"Well, Bob Cooley's '39 Ford was practicing going around the airfield to see if it was safe to drive home, when the fuel line broke and it caught on fire. We had no water out there. Now Bob's got no car. But to the best of my knowledge, it's nothing to do with any race."

"So how did the horse die then?" the big officer asked.

"Excuse me? Horse die? No horse died that I know of. What about you, General?" I shook my head. I looked at my brother and he did too. *Junior could go to work for Barnum and Bailey and probably own the company within a year*, I thought.

"Did something happen to Strawberry, Mrs. Larsen?" the big policeman said.

"Yes, something happened to her. She's lying out there on the runway, dead. What do you take us for, fools?"

"In all due respect to your age on top of all your motherhood, Mrs. Larsen, I think you are just a little worked up with the weather and it being Palm Sunday and everything. Easter week coming up. School's out. I'm sure Larry's horse is home safe in her stall right now. She sure isn't on the runway. We can go look if you want."

We rode in the back of the police car to the airfield. Ida Mae followed in her Chevy. They all had cigarettes going by the time we arrived. We walked around in the rain. The police looked at the burned-out Ford.

"Engine fire, like he said," the big officer said. "Where did you say the horse was lying?"

"Over here somewhere," Ida Mae said.

"And you saw the horse dead?" the little officer said.

"No, I didn't see her dead. I saw the horse alive, but I think her leg was broken and they were holding her down."

"We were trying to show Larry how to get the bridle back on right. He always put it on crazy. He is so short, we had to get her to lie down to show him. Then he got scared, because he said his mother would beat him, I guess he meant you, if he couldn't get it on right by this weekend. He said he was panicked and that's when he ran off with the horse and this wild story he told you. I am sorry to have to say this in front of you, Mrs. Larsen, because I respect you as a real mother, but what Larry said was one great big Fibber McGee. I'll bet Strawberry is home right now."

We rode in the police car to the Larsen's. The police officers looked around with their flashlights. There was no Strawberry. *Big surprise,* I thought.

"Well, we'll make a report, Mrs. Larsen," the little officer said. "If Strawberry shows up, please let us know. Otherwise, there isn't really too much else we can do tonight."

"And thank you all for your help. And particularly you, Mr. Malstrom," the big officer said. "So you're Junior huh? I have met your dad a number of times. He's on the school board, isn't he?"

"Yes, we all believe in education in our family," Junior Malstrom said.

"Well thanks a lot. I'm glad you helped us get this thing straightened out," the big officer said.

"Get what straightened out?" Ida Mae said.

"It looks like it's starting to rain again," my mother said. "You'll give us a ride back, officers?"

"Of course," the little officer said.

Ida Mae was already storming off toward the house.

"Ride this home," she yelled over her shoulder, giving us all the finger.

"That woman is a kind of a menace to society, isn't she?" my mother said.

"We shouldn't be too hard on her," Junior said. "Raising Larry must be a handful."

All of the adults nodded. My brother and I looked at each other and scratched our chins. *How did he do that? The Malstrom Guarantee was worth a lot more than I ever imagined. I wasn't even sure myself what happened anymore.*

@

"It's a campover," Bill Loon was explaining to my folks the next day. "We'll stay overnight and surf fish in the morning. Probably bring you home some nice fish for dinner."

"Exactly who all is going on this outing?" my mother said. "Your father?"

"Oh, sure. He'll be around, but he has a cold. He may not stay all night. It's usually pretty nippy out on the shore Easter week. It'll be me, Junior, my sister Mary Ann, and her friend Sherry Ferston. You know her, Ferston Redwood Shingles. Her dad's company. Maybe one or two others. You are welcome to join us."

"No," my mother said. "We don't want to join you. We're not Eskimos. Is that tonight or tomorrow night?"

"Tomorrow night," Bill Loon said, ducking his head a little in the doorway. "These ceilings are kind of low, aren't they?"

"The ceilings are fine. You just happen to be too tall for this type of architecture, which incidentally I designed myself. The good thing is you're young. Maybe you won't be so big when you are older." My father always smiled when he managed to create a little doubt and confusion in the mind of one of my friends. "Anyway, he can go, but his brother stays. We still don't know what happened to that horse. I don't want to lose them both on the same night."

"Agghh!" my mother said.

"I'm kidding," my father said.

"Well kid about something else."

❦

When I saw the beach late the next afternoon, it seemed different than I had remembered it. Maybe it was me that was different. I looked at the miles of pounding whitecaps and then as far as I could see in any direction, piled against the dunes—a thousand years of driftwood. It was as though this stretch of ocean had never been discovered by the white man.

Strawberry was stretched out near the shoreline, Jeep tracks leading away. Under her was a bizarre raft made from large random pieces of driftwood. It looked like Chris Craft's answer to the '39 Ford. It was held together with just enough rope to allow it to stay together until it was beyond the breakwater. Strawberry would be buried at sea. And no one knew about it except a few of us and the guy with the Jeep who was from Eureka and didn't know anyone except Junior Malstrom and his father.

Mary Ann had some hot soup on the open fire, and Sherry played on her Hawaiian ukulele, singing some popular songs and some we knew from school.

It was long after dark, at high tide, when Bill Loon went into the surf with his hip boots. He had set up a long iron spike in the sand with a block and tackle so he could easily pull the awkward vessel into the water when the tide surrounded it. He had poured gasoline from three two gallon cans all over the carcass. He had everything figured out somehow so that once the raft was afloat, all he had to do was pull the spike that held the winch system. He did it quickly and he was just in time, because the raft went right over the top of where he had been standing, past the whitecaps on its way out to sea.

We stood on the shore watching it bob and weave through the surf. The moon was about half full, so we could see it clearly. Mary Ann had hot chocolate by this time and the evening didn't seem as cold as it really was. That was when Sherry surprised us with a song nobody had ever heard. She found it in some old song book. It was about a race horse. She stood watching the raft and played softly as she strummed on the ukulele.

> Old Stewball was a race horse,
> and I wish he were mine.

He never drank water,
He always drank wine.

Mary Ann joined her in kind of a harmony. Their voices sounded really good together. It was a perfect song for a horse funeral.

Bill Loon strung his long hunting bow. He tested it with one arrow straight into the wind. He was satisfied and made some adjustments, as he called them, for the side winds and the spray off the surf. We walked to the receding shoreline. We each had an arrow that had a big wad of lighter fluid at the end.

Bill Loon lit the end of the first arrow and put it into his bow and pulled back as far as he could. The flaming arrow went high in the air and past the horizon. It got brighter as it went into the air and then fell into the ocean far to the right of the target.

"I've got the range now," he said.

The next three arrows landed right on the raft and ignited gasoline soaked driftwood. Strawberry was outlined by the flames, which were now blazing against the half-full moon. It looked like she was running sideways in the water beyond the whitecaps. Like she was in a race. The raft started coming apart after a while and the flames eventually started to die down. Soon the fire was gone and we knew that Strawberry was on her way to the bottom of the sea. We turned to walk back to the campfire.

@

The light from the moon illuminated the sand dunes. Along the top of one of them was an outline of people standing against the sky. They had been watching the burial. The group soon left, but in the distance we began to hear a familiar voice coming toward us. Junior Malstrom was mellow. I smiled as he approached. He walked up to me and gave me a hug, which made me realize that he smelled a little of alcohol. I had to smile again. I really appreciated what he had done to make good his guarantee, but even though I thought I would eventually talk again, right now I couldn't say anything.

"Your bike's safe, General. Too much heat right now. Wait a few days. We'll figure some way to say that you earned it."

"I thought this burial was going to be kept just among us," Bill Loon said, looking at Junior with his head cocked.

"Those were just some people who already knew the horse was dead anyway. They were either holding her down or were standing around when the General shot her. They wanted to see the raft and everything, so I thought sure, why not?"

"Did they pay?" Bill Loon asked.

"Sure, why not?"

"You never charge money for funerals," Bill Loon said. "It's bad luck."

"For regular funerals it is," Junior said. "But not for horse funerals. That's because there's not enough of them to really get any rules set."

"Like there are not too many rules for horse races with cars," Bill Loon said.

"Hardly any of those," Junior Malstrom grinned.

We all kind of laughed, because we knew that, in spite of all his craziness, Junior Malstrom was one-of-a-kind, as I guess we all were right then. Just kids in the wind.

"Hey Sherry, want to go to Arcata for a coke?"

"No, Junior. Didn't you know? I'm in love with General George Armstrong Custer."

Everyone laughed. Including me, but it was kind of embarrassing.

"How do you rate, Custer? You're not hardly twelve yet, are you? And you're camping with Sherry Ferston. She is a year older and will be in junior high next year. What are you going to do then? It doesn't matter. She'll be a movie star before she's out of high school, and we'll all be howling in the wind. I can't stay. I'm going into town tonight, but I want to leave you this. I've got another one, so have a great time tonight."

Junior gave us a pint of rum, which he had already taken more than a few swigs of. He also had three bottles of coke, which he handed over. We watched as he ran up a sand dune, waved at us and disappeared over the horizon.

Mary Ann immediately dumped the hot chocolate and started brewing some hot rum and cokes. Bill Loon put some more wood on the fire and then some more until we had a fire going several feet in the air. We all looked red and tanned as we sat around the flames, drinking from our tin cups of hot rum and coke. Sherry sang a few more songs and Mary Ann joined in. The rum was affecting the way I was thinking. Sherry was so good looking, I could hardly believe it. It didn't matter if it were night or day or in a windstorm or around a campfire. I made a little humming sound to myself. I was glad I would be able to talk again someday. It must be terrible not to be able to say anything for your whole life.

"Want to tell stories?" Mary Ann asked.

"Sure," Bill Loon said. "Who has one?"

"Why don't you tell that story about the hunter in the mountains that you read in Argosy? The one I heard you telling dad yesterday."

"You heard me telling that? I can't tell that one tonight. It's got a naked girl in it."

"Oh, sure, Bill. You can tell it. Is she really cute?" Sherry Ferston asked.

"Yep," Bill Loon said, nodding his head.

"How can you tell if she's cute if she doesn't have any clothes on?" I asked. Everybody looked at me. "Did I say something dumb?"

"Yes, but we are used to that. Did you forget? Those were the first words you said since yesterday." Sherry Ferston pulled me close to the fire, putting her hand inside my shirt.

"Tell the story, Bill, and let's find out exactly how cute your little naked girl is."

"Okay, but to start with, she's not mine and she's not little. She's a grown girl."

"So you mean she's fully developed?" Sherry asked. The rum was doing a funny thing.

"I don't know if she's fully developed," Bill said. "I don't know how you tell."

Bill Loon was out of his area of smartness, that's for sure. No wonder he didn't want to tell this story.

"Simple test," Sherry came back. "Does she jiggle?"

"I don't know. The story doesn't say."

"Then we'll just say she jiggles."

"Okay," Bill Loon said. "She jiggles."

He began the story. Nobody said a word until he was through. That story was so good, I didn't think I'd ever get my mind off thinking about nakedness ever again. I kept seeing the girl; she was actually a woman, naked, coming over the sand dunes with all the stolen jewelry around her neck and the .45 hidden in her hairdo, ready to kill the man who wanted her jewelry.

The rum was gone. We were glowing. Sherry whispered she thought it would be warmer and better if we were in the same sleeping bag. Cozier too. But I had to promise not to get fresh with her. *Right. Two in a bag? How could you keep from getting fresh? Stop breathing?* Then she whispered to me it would be all right, just for tonight. But I had to choose. Did I want to see or did I want to feel. I couldn't have both. I said I wanted to feel. She said she did too. Actually, I wanted to see, but it was so dark by then, I would have had to feel around to know what I was trying to see. That rum was something.

"Can we use your sleeping bag?" I asked. "If mine gets ripped, my mother might get suspicious."

"What was it like riding that race?" Bill Loon wanted to know, now that he knew I could talk again. I was kind of known for coming up with interesting ways of telling things. I was trying to write a few stories for the class at school.

"That would make a good story, you know."

"That can wait until tomorrow, right?" Sherry asked. "I'm kind of sleepy right now."

She was goofy, and she was lying about being sleepy, too. Once we got zipped in the bag, we took turns. We could feel anywhere we wanted, but only once in a certain place. And only for half a minute. It was so much fun, that we changed it by doubling the time to a minute. Then we gave the places bigger areas and then we decided we could go back, but we would have to go to another place in between. We called those visits reunions. It was during one of the reunions of hers that I fell asleep, breathing deeply and feeling no pain. The sound of the wind and the breakers continued right into my dreams. She was warm and strong, she was love, she was silky, she was smooth all over and she was not seamless. And what a sleeping bag. It didn't rip, it didn't stretch and it kept us warm all night long.

In the morning, with two poles cast into the surf, Bill Loon was ready to hear me tell about the race, but he smiled at me with the words "You and Sherry."

"She was cold," I said.

"Yep. The weather was pretty rough last night," he said. "You did the right thing for survival. Get warm."

I just nodded and looked out at the waves. Strawberry was out there bouncing along the bottom somewhere, scaring sea urchins. We looked over to the girls, cooking breakfast over the campfire. Mary Ann said something to Sherry and they both laughed and waved. Bill waved for them to come out to the shoreline.

"They'll want to hear when you tell the race," he said. "You are going to tell it, aren't you?" I nodded, still sleepy with the sea breeze blowing across my hair and face.

Pretty soon they brought us some bacon and eggs and toast and hot chocolate and put it on a blanket down where Bill had the two poles anchored in the sand. He had something on one of the lines. It seemed like Bill always had something on one of his lines.

"What were you laughing about over there just now?" he asked. They started laughing again.

"Nothing," Mary Ann said. And then they laughed again. "It was a riddle. Kind of stupid, but it made us laugh. That's all. Want to hear it? Okay. What did one strawberry say to the other strawberry? Give up? If we hadn't been in the same bed together, we wouldn't be in this jam now."

Bill Loon and I looked at each other and kind of laughed.

"I guess it's a lot funnier if you are cooking breakfast," Sherry said.

"The General is going to tell us about the race from where he was," Bill Loon said. "On top of Strawberry."

"Oh good, tell it," Mary Ann said. "And if you go blank, we'll chime right in, if we know something, won't we? It can be like a group story. Personally I almost peed my pants about three times before the race even got started."

"Mary Ann!" Sherry said.

"You know it's true," Mary Ann said. "But that could be another whole story."

"You want to start telling it now? While we're eating breakfast?" Sherry asked.

"Please please," Mary Ann said.

I thought for a minute. I saw Bill had a fish for sure. Probably a perch.

"Okay. I guess I'll start at the beginning of the race. It was last Sunday. It was Palm Sunday. We were going to be out of school for the week. It was about 2:30 in the afternoon, I think."

"That's right," Mary Ann said. "It was about 2:30. Good so far."

"Well, let's see. I walked Strawberry up to the starting line. She was really droopy, like she was up all night or something. Not like you Sherry. You always look good."

"Oh, please," Mary Ann said.

"Okay. Let's see, I remember I cupped my hand toward her ear so she would hear me. I was trying to stir her wild stuff up with some animal words that I got from this Tarzan funny book. I knew they sounded like a bunch of mumble mush to anyone but Tarzan and me, but they might help, so I tried them."

Kreeg-ah! Bundolo!

The Flying Boxcar

FLYING A KITE in the Fairhaven wind takes more work than a full-time job. And I mean any job. That's because there is more to know, it's trickier to do, it takes a deuce of a long time to learn, and to make matters worse, after you finally get your kite up, there's no paycheck to cash and it looks so perfect up there, nobody ever believes it was hard for you to begin with.

As the middle years were being stitched into our patchwork century of wars and social conformity, the kites of Fairhaven, always homemade works in progress, reflected a lust for something fresh and wild, something that was ours right up there next to the sun. That's why no two looked the same. The only thing they had in common was if they were strong, they were in the sky. If they weren't, they were in the bay.

Sometimes a certain kite, because of its special design and durability, would become locally famous. Bill Loon had one that was practically a legend. It was a huge box kite, covered with sail cloth, larger than anyone had ever seen. It had wood rails on the sides with plenty of bracing and understructure so it took all his strength along with extra help to launch it each time. He needed three others to lift and hold it in the air and all four of them would need to run like mad, hoping for a magic up gust of wind to get it into the air. Because it had a shelf on each side to attach things, he called it a cargo kite. Everyone else just called it the Flying Boxcar.

⊚

Jake Fowler said the blue kid, who had just moved to Fairhaven a week before, came from New Orleans, where he was born in the back of a Dairy Queen that was so cold he turned blue. But on the very first day that the Blue Hollar boy walked onto the playground before school, he held up his hand and said, "Hold it. I hear what you are sayin' about me. Somebody was misinfoamed."

The power that boy had when he raised his small blue hand was stunning. No one was even moving an eyelash when he started flipping words out all over everybody.

He told us he wasn't born in no New Orleans and didn't catch no blues from no Dairy Queen refrigerator. He said he was born just like he was with blue skin all over, in a place called Blue Hollar, where some of his cousins had the same malady. A lot of people there were shy, but frisky, he said, so they didn't usually go very far to get married. That's how a lot of them ended up that way. Pure blue. Around his part of the country they called them hillbilly bluebloods or more often just the blue people. We continued to stand in amazement as he told us how he happened to travel to New Orleans and what he saw there.

He said that his stepdad, a man named Scuttles, was not blue. He was a carney who had kidnapped him from his mother when he was six years old and taken him on the road to be with him in the circus. He hated it, but years went by and when he was old enough, he began running away. Once he ran away when they were doing the show in New Orleans. He was hiding one day while his stepdad was scouring the streets for him. He was nervously humming "God Bless America" for some reason he couldn't remember, when he saw what looked like a thousand people coming down the street singing and playing trumpets. They were all dressed so strangely, he got in the parade and walked along. He figured his stepdad could never pick him out of this group. Even though he was blue, he was small and not really noticeable beside all these colorful characters. At first he thought it was a big coronation like they had in England to celebrate a new queen.

"But then I see the guy up ahead that they's celebratin' about and he's deader than a crucified pin cushion. Let me outa this nut patrol, I'm thinkin', but then I see my stepdad Scuttles over by the garbage cans I was just at, and he's lookin' around and behind them with his two dogs. They are gettin' all mixed up because of the garbage smells. I keep my eyes on the road ahead and he never notices me.

"After a bit, I start chimin' in with their singin' of 'The Saints Go Marchin' In' and pretend I'm happy just like everyone else. I catch another view of this wagon up ahead that's bein' pulled by two horses clickin' along together. The person they was celebratin' is laid out like pheasant under glass, but it was mysterious, because they were singin' and dancin' in all directions like it was the happiest day of the guy's life. And it was his dang funeral.

"I figured out right then and there that if people think there's as dang much to celebrate being dead as being alive, it's probably because they haven't tried being dead yet."

I had to think about that.

"If this was their dead parade, how would they find a live parade to top it? They'd have to throw the guy into the air and fly him around on flags," he told us.

Jake Fowler looked a little worried about this Blue Hollar boy. He was afraid there was something supernatural going on and didn't want to badger him too much for fear of getting some kind of curse leveled at him. Even so, his natural instinct for running board humor kept him moving forward with questions.

"This blue place you come from, it's on earth, right?" Jake asked. Nobody laughed. Jake squirreled his lips in a little wince.

"Georgia," the Blue Hollar boy said.

"Is it some place religious? Are the people there, you know, like that way?" Jake asked.

"You mean like the garden in the first book of Bible heaven? Hell, no siree, just the opposite. Where I come from, they believe when the Lord rested on the seventh day, well that was his big mistake. He should have been drainin' the swamp. And people don't forget a thing like that. Particularly after 2000 years and their grandkids are still standin' in it."

"So you come from a place called the Swamp?" Jake asked, feeling a little braver.

"Now that would be pretty ignorant, wouldn't it?" the Blue Hollar boy said. "There's a thousand swamps around there. You'd spend a year tryin' to find the right one. It's just called Blue Hollar."

"Why holler? Is everybody so deaf they got to yell?" Jake asked.

I got the sense that he was asking for trouble.

"They hear just fine. It's that the place is set down in a clearing, like a slope. It might seem like a hole in the ground, if ye didn't know better. That's a hollar, see? You're thinkin' I can't hear you, so you holler. That ain't it. It ain't full anymore, so now it's hollar. That's it. Same word, different idea."

Jake Fowler looked up at a lone seagull being blown out toward the mouth of the bay. Maybe he was thinking of being with it. He had no further questions.

Then the Blue Hollar boy started talking very low, like we were around a campfire in the forest. We started coming in, leaning closer to hear him better.

"And that swamp itseff ain't the only devilment. They got Cottonmouth. They're deadly snakes, you know. And they got malaria carryin' skeeters, and more people are being born blue like it's a dread disease spreading a plague over the land."

Then he took off his coat, pulled his shirt sleeve high on his arm and suddenly tree-snapped his double jointed elbow straight out at us backwards, fingers wide.

"True Blue!" he suddenly shouted.

Everyone jumped back. You didn't run across a kid like this very often. He was so small and thin, some boys might want to try to pick on him. But after hearing him, and watching his arm snapping like a branch, any sane bully would believe he was best left alone.

"You don't have to flinch. It ain't catchy," he said laughing a little heh, heh, hee.

Even though he was friendly and funny, he was kind of scary too, because he was hard to look at, being blue and everything. One girl, Marsha, who always claimed to be studying the Bible, wouldn't look directly at him.

"Will people turn to salt if they look at you?" she asked.

"Will they turn to sugar if they look at you?" he asked right back.

"Of course not," Marsha said. "But you are different."

"Okay, let's find out. Strike a pose you would like to be in for the rest of your life and then look right in my eyes." The Blue Hollar boy said.

"No!" Marsha yelled and covered her eyes.

"Don't be afraid, Marsha," Jake Fowler said. "Turning you to salt would be an improvement."

A few kids laughed, but most were already looking at the Blue Hollar boy through their fingers with their eyes squinting almost shut. Some even ran for the safety of the lupines. Marsha's brother decided to look right at the sun, saying he would rather be struck blind than turn to salt. Sister Marsha smacked him on the back of his head with her Bible, and he went flying face first into the sand. When he got up, he saw the front of his shirt and felt his gritty face. He thought he was already turning to a pillar of salt and started running home crying until somebody stopped him.

The bell monitor rang our modified cowbell to come into class. There were thirty kids in Rolph Elementary school that year. Fifteen of them were first and second graders. They were in the east room. Fifteen of us were in the west room, third grade through the sixth. Each grade had its separate row. Jake and I were in the fifth grade. Sherry Ferston and Mary Ann Loon were in the sixth grade. I sat across from Sherry. Jake was in front of me next to Mary Ann, who wanted to be a schoolteacher when she grew up. She already knew all the parts of speech when most of the kids didn't know speech had any parts at all.

We all ran in, put our lunch pails on the shelf in the back and took our places. The Blue Hollar boy came in last.

"And who are you?" Miss Nickols asked, eyes wide. He handed her a note from his mother and some traveling papers, which she read over carefully. She soon announced that the new boy would be in the fourth grade. That meant that he would be in the fourth grade row along with Marsha and two others. He asked if it was all right if he sat in the back of the class for a few days, which was good thinking on his part, because hardly anybody would be able to concentrate on school work if they could see him. The only one that would have him head on all day would be Miss Nickols and if she kept forgetting what lesson we were on, that was all right with us.

❡

Like a lot of things that took getting used to on the spit, we got used to being around the Blue Hollar boy. He was known as Mr. Odekirk for the first few days. That's the way Miss Nickols did it if you were new. She pretended like you just stepped off the upper deck of the Queen Mary from a North Atlantic cruise. Then after letting you get cocky and comfortable for a while, like you were related to King Farouk or something, she would start calling you by your first name. That's when you got officially bounced out of first class and joined the rest of us sweating away down in steerage.

"Well, Mr. Odekirk, I guess we can start calling you Odin, if that would be all right with you."

"No it would not. I do not like my given name, Miz Nickol," the Blue Hollar boy said.

"That's just like me. When I was your age, I didn't like my name either. I tried nicknames, but none of them stuck. I finally went back to it."

"I plan on goin' back too. Not to my name, but back to Georgia one day and find the skunk that came up with that name and told it to my mother. I do believe I will kill him with my bare hands!"

"Ouch. Okay. We'll get another name for you. What would you like to be called?"

"How about Casper?" Jake said. Everyone gasped and hissed, because that was pretty hard-biting, even for Jake.

"Casper's fine," the Blue Hollar boy said. "He's that ghost, right? That would be like being named after a movie star."

"A cartoon movie star," Jake said.

Everyone laughed.

Miss Nickols thought a minute and said "We are not calling you Casper. How about Odie?"

Everyone laughed again.

"What are you laughing at now?" Miss Nickols was getting red around the gills.

"It sounds like he eats oats," Jake said.

"Well, what do they call you at home?"

"Most people don't like it, but my mother calls me Bluper. Combination of blue and diaper I guess."

People had tears in their eyes from laughing.

"Oh, for heaven's sake. We are not calling you Bluper either," Miss Nickols said. "Odekirk. How about Kirk?"

"Kirk or Casper or Bluper," he said. "Whatever you vote is fine to me." Everyone in the class shouted "Kirk," and that's how the Blue Hollar boy got his new name, Kirk.

Sherry Ferston leaned across the aisle and touched my arm. "He looks like a little blue angel," she said.

"Let's start our lesson," Miss Nickols said. "Kirk, do you know the answer to yesterday's first history question?"

"How would I know it? I wasn't here."

"Oh, that's right. Okay. It's what year did Columbus discover America?"

"Yes. I may have it, Miz Nickel. It's 1492, I reckon."

"Is that correct, Mary Ann?" Miss Nickols asked. Because of her interest in becoming a school teacher, Miss Nickols made her a kind of assistant, mostly a kind of word and number patrol.

"Yes, it is," Mary Ann said with her history book opened to the Discovery of America.

Big deal. Everybody knows that. It's in the poem.

"So that's correct, Kirk. Did you memorize that from your last school?" Miss Nickols asked.

"It's easy for me to recall that I guess, because there wudn't too much else happenin' that year 1492."

"Oh there was stuff happening. It's just that there ain't that many people that could write back then," Jake said.

"Jake, raise your hand if you want to say something, and please make it relevant to the lesson," Miss Nickols said.

"And ain't *is not* in the dictionary," Mary Ann said, raising her hand as she spoke.

She was getting to be a pain.

Jake raised his hand.

"Okay Jake. What relevant point do you have? The date of the second voyage perhaps? The whereabouts of some of the lost documents?"

"Heck no. I was just thinking. Picture this: Indian Charlie here, red; me, white; and Kirk here, blue in an oil painting called "The Discovery of the All-American Boys: Red White and Blue." There was a silence.

"Jake, leave the class. Go stay in the PTA room until I get there."

"Why? For being an American?" Jake asked on the way out.

"No, for, well for not being relevant. Just leave." Miss Nickols said.

"For being a jerkhead," Marsha said.

"Jerkhead ain't in the Bible, Marsha," Jake said.

"And ain't ain't in the dictionary," Marsha said.

Jake went out, half-smiling, and shut the door behind him. He had been sent out of class before. He was used to it.

"Miz Nickols?" Kirk asked.

"Yes, Kirk. I'm truly sorry. That must be awful for you. And you too, Charlie."

"Miz Nickols. I think Jake is real confused. Would it help if I went into the PTA room and had a little talk, maybe straighten out a few mysteries for him?"

Little blue Kirk actually stretched his arms and cracked his knuckles like he was getting ready to pound somebody. Miss Nickols told him it was okay if he wanted to go talk to Jake, but there was to be no fighting. As Kirk walked out the door she quickly added, "And watch yourself. Jake can be tricky."

Fifteen minutes later the two of them came back in. Jake didn't look very tricky. He looked more like he had been dragged across the Dead Sea and had to swim back through the bodies. Jake apologized to Charlie and to everyone and then announced that he had a new friend, Kirk. He had invited him to go and watch the kites fly on Saturday. Miss Nickols landed in her chair, jaw loose and looking up in the air like she was getting a transfusion.

"Okay, what did he say to you, Jake?"

"Well, Kirk reached in his pocket and pulled out four spoons and started clicking a rhythm while he talked. He said he didn't want any enemies. He said he didn't know how long he had to live so he wanted to only have friends. And he kept clicking until I didn't know if I was alive or asleep or what. I was just staring into his eyes. Then he suddenly stopped clicking and said 'So do you want to be my friend or is this the room you want to die in?' I jumped awake and laughed so hard I had to go to the boys' room. When I came back to the PTA room, I asked if he would put the spoons away before he turned me into a zombie and that's when we both laughed and that's when I invited him to come see the kites fly on Saturday. And that's also when I told him I would be his friend for as long as he ever wanted."

Miss Nickols walked toward Jake and looked at him carefully. She sensed he was telling the truth. She asked Kirk if that is what happened. He said it was pretty much what happened all right. She asked about the spoons. Kirk said it was what he played in the side show he did at the circus. He learned to talk at the same time he was playing them as part of the entertainment. Miss Nickols asked if he would show the class, so he did. While he was clicking along, hitting the spoons against his knees, he leaned his little back against Miss Nickols desk. When he was through, she asked him why he said he wasn't going to live very long. She didn't like it when children talked like that, she said. He got into some fancy rhythms with the spoons again and started explaining while he played. Then he suddenly stopped, holding the spoons at his side.

He said he didn't mean to scare anybody about dying, but blue people like him usually didn't live very long lives, because they sometimes had other things wrong with them besides being blue.

He clicked the spoons again and went on to say he had another big problem. The one he told us about before on the playground. He had been kidnapped by his stepdad when he was very young and made to travel with him and be in the circus. He was known as the Penguin Boy, raised by penguins. Scientists had found him at the South Pole in the middle of a big group of penguins and brought him back to the United States. He said it wasn't true, that the whole thing was made up.

"The circus story or the penguin story?" Miss Nickols wanted to know.

"The circus story is true. The penguin story is complete hogwash. I was never raised by penguins," Kirk said.

Before that penguin story was concocted, he said he was The Polar Bear Boy, raised by polar bears. Scientists had found him at the North Pole in that show, but people could tell it was phony. A polar bear would eat him, they said. They booed him off the stage and tried to tar and feather his stepdad Scuttles for taking their money. People would yell up at him, "How did you learn to talk like that at the North Pole? From polar bears? We think you are lying." He said he cried a lot at night until they changed the act to The Penguin Boy.

With him coming from the South Pole it was easy to say "That's why he has his southern accent." It was stupid, he said, because no one lived on the South Pole, but everyone laughed and liked it. They had three penguins for the show. One was supposed to be his mother. He could never remember which one. The other two were his uncles. His penguin dad had supposedly been killed in the Iceberg Wars. He had to dive into cold water each show and swim with them. Then he would sit on a rock that had a heater under it and play the spoons like he was talking to them in Penguin while somebody on the accordion would play a medley of songs like "In the Cool, Cool, Cool of the Evening," "Baby, Its Cold Outside," and stuff like that.

The audiences loved it, but he hated it so he tried to escape whenever he had the chance. However, his stepdad always found him and brought him back. He had to rent these special hunting hounds the last two times in order to find him. He finally just bought the two dogs and tied them outside his trailer in case Kirk ever tried to escape again. But Kirk put sleeping pills from his stepdad's medicine cabinet with some hamburger and the hounds never woke up until he was well away and hiding in the alleys of New Orleans. After he escaped by marching in the dead man's parade, he caught a train home to his mother.

"Why did he do that to you?" Marsha asked.

"Why? Money," he said. "The coin of the realm. That's in the Bible there, isn't it? Render unto Caesar?" Marsha turned red and started pretending to leaf through her Bible. "It was a lot of money, too. I was pretty much the main attraction. Except for the 'All-Natural Mermaid. Men Only.' That one made a lot of money too."

"What was that show like?" Jake asked.

"Well, I never seed it. They wouldn't let kids in. But I queried this here man one time that was on his way out if the show was good. He declared it was. Real good, he said. I asked him what made it so good. He said that for one thing the fin didn't go up that high."

Everyone looked at each other. Some put their hand over their mouth. Marsha put her hands over her ears. Miss Nickols asked Kirk to stick to the story, but I don't think she knew what the story was anymore so she didn't stop him.

I realized I was hearing the most bizarre show-and-tell time I had ever been to. Nobody would want to tell about their new socks after this.

"Anyway, I finally got back to my mum. We left that day. She said we were in the southeast and we should travel just as far as we could to the northwest and that might throw my stepdad off. That was the plan, so we drove for days until we wound up here. Found it by mistake, yes'm. It was at the end of the road and not on the map. This here Fairhaven is pretty out of the way. We figured this was a good place to hide out."

"You think your stepdad might find you here?" I asked.

"He's got a powerful amount of determination," Kirk said. "He might well could."

"What's he look like?" someone asked.

"Well, there's one good question. He drives a pickup truck like a lot of them parked across the way there at the plywood plant. It'd likely have a couple of big hounds chained to the bed. Georgia plates. He wears an old cow hat, mustache, chews a lot of tobacco, a plug or two at a time. If he gets out of the cab, don't get too close. He can pop you so fast, nobody'll even see it. They'll think you slipped and fell. He'll even be so bodacious as to pretend to help you up and whap, you get another one. And he don't mind if he lays his hounds on you neither. They'll tear the clothes right off ya. And he won't bat an eye. He wants his meal ticket back and he dudn't care how. If he can't take me back for the show, he'd as soon kill me. He told me that, face to face. But I'm not that worried. I think you'd have to be blind, drivin' drunk with a broken arm and one leg to end up here!"

Kirk smiled, but no one smiled with him for the first time since he started talking. Not meaning to, he had sort of insulted us.

"*You* got here, didn't you?" Jake said. He was starting to get his natural self back.

"You sure got a point there, Jake," he said. "We all ended up here some way or t'other, didn't we? I'm happy I found this place."

Everyone smiled again. It was real easy to like this blue kid.

Someone asked if he would play the spoons some more. Miss Nickols agreed that would be nice. He hopped up on Miss Nickols desk, sitting, and started playing again. He looked to me like a river skeleton, tree roots in spring, when they shimmer for a short time with the rush of melting water, just before they snap into the stream. Sherry had my arm again, touching it all up and down as she watched Kirk.

"He is so precious," she whispered as she turned and looked right into my eyes. All the spelling words for the test that day suddenly erased from my memory. I would have to go over them again. I didn't care. I knew I was half crazy, but Sherry was worth it.

Kirk said we could ask questions while he played. That's what he used to do in the show. One of the kids asked him about being blue. He said blue was okay, but he wanted to do something different, not just be something different. He wanted to do something so different that maybe nobody ever did it before. Did he wish he wasn't blue? He answered that question like it was a poem, almost with a tune.

"Do I want to be blue / Blue as a day in summer. Yea / sometimes I do / sometimes I don't / depends on the day / my body is light / my body is fast / and it ain't much good except for lookin' at / and floatin' away / whenever the time comes / I'll be ready / yea."

"He grabs your attention like a vice grips," I whispered to Sherry. She just looked straight in my eyes like she didn't hear a thing I was saying, but I thought I knew what she was thinking. This kid was beyond anything we had ever seen.

Kirk hopped off the desk and walked around the room playing. Some kids were clapping in time. Now he was like a little blue jellyfish as he moved back to his seat. He stood and rolled out a final, wild clicking noise.

"Are there any other questions?" Miss Nickols asked. Her eyes were moist and kind of red.

Sherry raised her hand.

"Ahhm, choking a little there. Sorry Kirk," she said. "I want to give you a special invitation. Would you play spoons in our PTA talent show? Solo or maybe a duet with a piano? I would really like it. I think we all would."

He gave another little spoon roll and then clicked along while he talked.

"Your beauty is a tune / forever around us / a wish fulfilled / and it would be my honor / to do your biddin' anytime you want / I will be here for you / just say the word," he said, and then finished with another roll of the spoons. Everyone clapped. Sherry reached across the aisle, looking at me and gripping my hand. She moved her lips like she was saying something to me. It was three words I couldn't make out, but I think the middle one was love.

This guy is in the fourth grade? Where did he learn to talk like that? It must have been in the sideshow because I never heard anything to beat it.

After a long silence, Miss Nickols asked us to get our essay books out and write about this morning or anything else in the whole wild world we really cared about, and to do it without stopping for the next fifteen minutes. Pencils were in the air before she finished speaking.

"Psst. *Anything?*" Jake Fowler whispered across the room to Miss Nickols.

"Anything, Jake. That's what I said," Miss Nickols called back to him.

"Because I wanted to write about the Mermaid Show," he called back in his loud whisper.

"I'm not surprised," Miss Nickols said.

Jake showed up to see the kites on Saturday morning with Kirk, just like he said he would. Kirk was quieter and looked smaller than in school, but he was still a big hit. With the wind in his light hair, he looked like he could be blown away in a quick gust. Once there, the older boys overshadowed Jake's grammar school bravado, and he faded into the background. He went to work getting his kite ready for flight. Bill Loon took an interest in Kirk and said he was so special it was like having a good luck charm for a friend.

Junior Malstrom thought he might be good luck too. He was willing to take him on the road as a fundraising spokesman for the cold and hungry. Phony, of course. He thought they could make a lot of money and split it fifty-fifty. Sherry Ferston started beating Junior with her fists, so he put a hold on the plans. Kirk wasn't fazed by any of this but rather had some funny things to say about most of it. Then he went to Sherry who sat him on her knees while she sat on a small stool. They talked about the PTA talent show.

Did I have competition? I didn't think so. Kirk was about forty pounds and only in the fourth grade.

Because they were in Junior High and didn't know the whole story, I told Bill and Junior about Kirk and his bad stepdad, Scuttles. Bill looked kind of quiet and stared off to the sand dunes and then down the road. He didn't look worried or anything. He was just doing an inventory to see that everything on the peninsula was in its place. At least that's what I figured. Junior kind of smiled while he stood next to him and looked around.

"Scuttles, huh? Be kind of interesting if a guy like that came around," Junior said.

"Don't ask for trouble," Bill Loon said. "Enough seems to find you anyway."

The rest of the guys began to get their kites in the air, but it was difficult as usual. A lot of yelling, swearing, crashing, ripping of paper and cloth. Even so, by 10:30 the sky was full of color. Everyone settled in to watch what we thought would be the big event of the day: the launching, once again, of Bill Loon's Flying Boxcar.

Bill Loon said the original idea for the Boxcar was to make drop shipments across the bay. No one knew why. The Ferry cost 15 cents (5 cents for kids) and you could take as much stuff with you as you wanted. Whether it was carrying anything or not, the Flying Boxcar was so spectacular, few people who ever saw it for the first time thought it was a kite. It looked more like a clubhouse. It had only flown a few times before this Saturday, so everyone was looking forward to it. It always took a strong, steady wind to get it up and so we waited.

After about a half hour of watching the kites, I spotted a shiny black '51 Ford pickup driving toward us down the hog fuel road that leads to the bay. I thought it was a mill worker going for stove wood along the bayshore. It wasn't. Chained in the back of the truck were two huge dogs. I turned to tell Bill Loon, but he had already seen it. The truck stopped. My throat locked. A man stretched his arms as he got out of the truck and looked at the kites in the sky. Not interested in them, he came across the path that cut through the big field of lupines toward us. His smile was orange with the worst teeth I had ever seen. I turned to warn Kirk, but he was already gone, probably slipped under the green foliage into the acres of lupines. He could be anywhere within a matter of minutes. The man waved and called out that he thought his son might be out here playing. He was looking for him.

"Who's your son?" Bill Loon asked.

"Cain't miss'em. Odekirk. He's blue," the man said, showing more orange as he got closer. He had a mustache, leather hat and a cheek full of juice that leaked out the corner of his mouth. The kids from school tried to look like they didn't know anything, but it only made it worse. It was obvious they were hiding something and they were scared.

"The only thing we got blue around here is the ocean," Junior Malstrom said.

The man didn't look like anyone's dad or even stepdad when he got near us. He looked like death. He just needed a hood and one of those wood things to whack the wheat with. His thin, gray eyes scanned the lupines. The dogs in the back of the pickup were barking like crazy. Everyone just stared in different directions like we were in one of those old photographs.

"Did you say blue? That's kind of different. How tall is he?" Junior finally said after a tense silence. He pretended to be helping a kid having trouble with his kite.

"Who cares how tall he is, Shorty, he's blue! You either seen him or you ain't so save your crap for the next guy," the man said and blew an orange wad from the corner of his mouth, which carried out across the lupines.

Junior had his work cut out for him.

"You're right. Who cares? Ain't seen him anyway," Junior said.

"What about the rest of you?" he yelled. "He's here in these green bushes here, hain't he? Under here somewhere, hain't he? Dang all y'all. I'll bet these $200 worth of huntin' dogs could find him real fast if I cut'em loose. They could find him anywhere on this here peninsula if I went and got a shirt or something of his. You'll all be better off jest tellin' me."

"They cain't dang find what dang hain't here," Junior said, making fun of the man's accent. "I don't keer if you did pay $100 for them."

"Ah said $200! You a retard?" the man said.

"That's what I thought you said. Wharn't sure. We kin help ye look, mebbe," Junior said. "How much you payin'? We ain't doin' much. Jes flyin' kites. How long ago you see him? Maybe he ain't blue anymore."

"He's always blue, dickhead," the man spit again. "Look, I don't want no bogus search party. Here's ten dollars to anyone who seen him and sez where he went."

Marsha grabbed the ten-dollar bill right out of his hand.

"Where he go, girl?" the man went after her.

"I think he went that way," she pointed toward the bay. "He just was here and then went invisible under the lupines. That's probably where he went. I wouldn't go after him though. He could turn you to salt if he wanted."

"Give me my ten dollars back. You'll get it when I find him," the man said as he grabbed Marsha and landed with her on the ground.

Junior kicked the man in the side of the head with one of his engineer boots. It had to hurt. The man rolled over holding his ear.

"Hey trench mouth. You're through here," Junior said. "She told you what she knew. Leave your money and clear out. We ain't bothering you, and you don't know how lucky that is for you," Junior said.

"Why you sawed off little . . ."

Bill Loon tripped the man as he lunged at Junior. They had practiced it a lot, and because of Junior's nature, they had to use it a lot too. They were good at it. The man fell right at Junior's feet.

"Get up real slow so I can check that you're not bleeding too much out of your ear, there," Junior said. "Then get out. And don't ever come back or you will wish you had never been born, never had a son, and never set foot in Fairhaven. You can quote me on that. And you can trust me. I am giving it to you straight. You are in the wrong place for trying to be a bully. You know what they call us on the mainland? The ghost killers in the wind."

Junior was too much. Nobody called us that. Bill Loon was kind of shaking his head and smiling grimly. Sherry stood next to me, holding my arm while Mary Ann was holding Sherry's on the other side. Marsha was still on the ground with her ten-dollar bill.

The man got up, picked up his leather hat and started walking toward his truck. He turned to look at us, like he was figuring out who to kill first.

"I'm coming back," he said. "And I'll have a piece of his clothes. These hounds will find him no matter where he is. If he was here in the last month, they can trace him."

The man got in his truck, turned around and his tires ripped through the hog fuel as he left for the main road.

Kirk came leaping out of the lupines about fifty feet away. He was frightened; he didn't even look like the same person. Even his blue was a sort of purple for a time.

"Those dogs'll find me sure," he said. "They can track a flea in an ant farm. He's killed people. I know. The dogs too. They even killed a wild boar once. And that ain't easy. I know he already found where we live. He's gonna come back with something of mine from the house. He's already found where we live."

"Is he alone?" Bill Loon asked.

"Just him and the dogs," Kirk said.

"Too bad for him. Where's your mom?" Junior asked.

"Arcata. She works as a waitress. Odd hours. Can we get the police?"

"No phones. Besides they'd never make it in time," Junior said. "Your place is up in Finn town, right?"

"Yep. I could walk it in twenty minutes."

"Then he'll be back in twenty," Bill Loon said.

"Dogs can't trace over water. Could we put him on a boat?" I asked. *I was sorry the minute I said it.*

"Do you see anybody here with a boat, Custer?" Junior asked me. "This is the kite club; it ain't the yacht club."

"I cain't go back with him," Kirk said. "I'd soon as die."

"Not today, blue guy," Junior said. "Nobody here dies today. Give me one of your socks, Kirk. I'll lead the hounds straight to Cannoli's house. I'm taking care of Nippers while they're away."

"Nippers? The Cannoli's Doberman?" Mary Ann asked. "That dog is deadlier than those hounds."

"No he's not. Once you get to know him," Junior said. "Oh, he'd kill probably, but not if he likes you. He's not like regular Dobermans. The ones they say turn on their masters. He's not like that."

"You can't fool those hounds," Kirk said. "They'll still smell me stronger than that sock and come right for me."

"I have an idea," Bill Loon said. We all looked toward him. "How much do you weigh?" He asked.

"Not much," Kirk said.

"That's good," Bill Loon said. "Do you mind if I heft you for a second?"

"What for?" Kirk asked.

"I want to see how much you weigh. I've got an idea that might solve our hound problem."

"Okay," Kirk said.

Bill Loon picked Kirk up and nodded. "It could work. Let me carry you over here," he said. He carried him with Kirk practically sitting on one hand to the Flying Boxcar, which stood next to a clearing in the sand. It was the stretch that was used as the runway to launch the big kite.

"What in tarnation is this? A circus outhouse?" Kirk asked.

"No. It's a big kite," Bill Loon said. "You can't be more than about forty-five pounds. Can you fit in there?" Bill lifted Kirk over the top and helped him get settled on the wood structure in the corner. It had a triangular shelf, which he sat on, and wood footing where he placed his feet. He was so small that he actually fit in one corner of the kite. It was the corner that had the rag-tied tail flowing from it.

"Are you afraid of heights?" Sherry asked.

"I've stood on the hills in Tennessee before," Kirk said.

"Okay. It will be like sitting on a very high hill in Tennessee, but there won't be any hill," Bill Loon said. "If you don't want to do it, just say it, but I think it will work."

"What are you going to do?" Kirk asked.

"We are going to put you up in the cargo kite over the bay," Bill Loon said. "The dogs will have no idea you're up there. You can sit there pretty comfortable. I'll tie your waist to the side frame with a slip knot so you won't blow off. You can untie it if you need to. Can you swim?"

"I used to swim with the penguins, but it was a little pool."

"Are you sure you want to do this?" Bill asked.

"Hellzapoppin' no! I ain't sure at all! Go up in a kite? I hain't even had time to be considerin' it. I just don't know what else to do."

"You'll be the first person to fly in a kite over Humboldt Bay. Kind of like being a pioneer or explorer, if we can get you up," Bill Loon said with a look of determination on his face.

"Can you get me down? That's the question I'm thinkin' on," Kirk said.

"The line I use for the cargo kite is more than 200-pound test deep sea fishing line. It'll hold. If we get you up, there is no logical reason we can't get you down," Bill Loon said.

The wind started blowing steady. Bill Loon arranged to have five of us boys hold the back of the kite up. We could lift it okay, but it would take quite a run to get it into the air. Junior started jumping around telling Bill that he was crazy to put a kid up in a kite.

"Okay, Kirk, you are going to need to control the spin by lifting or letting out the tail here," Bill Loon said, paying no attention to Junior.

"The spin?" Kirk asked. "It's gonna spin?"

"Not that much," Bill said. "It's just a figure of speech."

"It's not a figure of speech. It's a direct verb," Mary Ann said.

"It's okay. I'll do it," Kirk said. "I can think of worse things happenin' to me right now. Let's go before I change my mind."

"Wrap this around you," Sherry said, handing him a small blanket. "It will be cold up there. Come back safe."

"If the kid falls, it's on your head, Bill. You and the blue kid will both be dead in the water. Why do it?" Junior asked.

"To save his life," Bill Loon said. "You know it and I know it, Junior. That man. That stepdad Scuttles. He's a crazy man. You saw it in his eyes. There was death there. He's even got a shotgun. We aren't going to be able to trip him with our little trick again."

"You're right. You got me. I see your point. Now I just wish I would have thought of it," Junior said, smiling. "You get him up in the air and I'll take care of the dogs with this sock."

"You are going to be safer up there than we are down here," Bill Loon said in his steady voice. "I trust the kite more than I trust that outlaw stepdad of yours."

"Okay. Me too," Kirk said.

I couldn't believe how brave the little blue guy was.

"Here's a thermos of hot chocolate," Mary Ann said. "But don't open it, until the kite stops the deep looping."

"Deep looping?" Kirk said, his blue eyes shot in all directions with excitement. "This is gonna be some ride."

Junior Malstrom ran Kirk's sock all around the bushes, but nowhere near Bill Loon, and then stuck it so it hung out of his shoe as he ran in a circle pattern toward the Cannoli house.

While Bill Loon had us all lined up, holding the Flying Boxcar off the ground, Kirk huddled in one corner, rope around his waist lashed to the side frame. We all started running, slowly at first and then as fast as we could until the kite was in the air. I fell face-forward just as it went airborne. It didn't look anywhere near as big once it was flying over the bay. Its blue and gray-white camouflage colors made it look like it belonged in the sky.

The kite went higher and higher. Kirk was yelling louder than Lou Costello, calling "AAAbbottt!" in his little voice as the big kite swayed and dipped over the whitecaps. He was afraid, but alive and underway. Soon the kite was up near the low clouds that were passing swiftly by. Except for the seagulls taking curious sweeps toward it, the Flying Boxcar was barely noticeable from the ground unless you looked right up at it.

Kirk had finally settled in and was leaning back against the frame of the kite and waving to us. He was able to control the kite by pulling on the tail, letting it in and out.

"Here comes Jones!" someone shouted.

The truck was travelling twice as fast as before, hog fuel flipping out behind. The man jumped out with the truck's engine still running. The dogs, on leather leads, jumped out of the cab after him. His free hand grabbed a shotgun.

"Daddy's come to take you home, baby blue!" he said and a plug of juice flew out of his mouth into the air. He gave the dogs a big sniff of a little dirty T-shirt, then tucked it back in his jacket. They pulled hard on the leads straight in our direction. "Last chance, you little sand rats! Where is he? Where is my sweet little Penguin Boy?" Nobody said a word. "Okay. You ast for it!" He let the dogs off the leads.

They were maniacs. The two of them ran right up and back and around us, knocking half of us to the ground. None of them went near Bill Loon who was standing a ways away. The sock trick worked except that the dogs tore a few coats and practically snorted us to death. Some kids were crying and crawling around. Nobody wanted to stand up again. Bill Loon looked over, with the Flying Boxcar on the other end of his reel of heavy fish line. He wanted to help, but there was nothing he could do without letting go of his precious blue cargo. The dogs moved around the bushes, just like Junior had done and started running in circles toward the Cannolis' place, about a quarter mile down the road.

The dogs were well in the distance before we dared to look up. Against the morning sun, Kirk blended in with the blue and white painted parts of the Flying Boxcar. But we could all make out his form and saw that, in spite of whatever that ride must've been like, he was drinking Mary Ann's hot chocolate.

"General, would you do me a favor and hold on to this kite here for a second?" Bill Loon said to me. "My arms are tired. I've got to shake them out for a second or so," Bill Loon said.

I didn't want to get caught holding a kite 150 feet in the air with a kid lashed to the other end. I almost got lynched for a screwball horse race a few weeks before.

Then we heard it. Our heads all turned. A shotgun blast. Then another.

"He killed Junior!" Mary Ann screamed.

We waited. Bill Loon handed me the large mounted reel that held the kite and before I knew it, it was in my hands. In spite of all my effort, the kite pulled me through several yards of lupine bushes, flowers flying in all directions, before I could get a footing. It was enough rest for Bill Loon's arms just to swing them around in the air for a minute and so he took the giant reel back from me before long.

I was okay. My hands were still connected. Sherry looked at me and smiled as she looked at my hands. There were some creases and two bent fingers, but I was fine.

Finally, after what seemed like forever, we saw the tiny, bobbing outline of Junior Malstrom walking toward us like Charlie Chaplin. He was waving an all-clear sign and Bill Loon began immediately to reel Kirk in. All of our eyes were skyward as Kirk began the careful but treacherous descent back to the ground.

Junior Maelstrom began telling us what had happened at the Cannolis. Their wood fence was nearly seven feet tall, but Junior was inside, standing next to the house with Nippers by the collar. The man fired both barrels through a knot hole to scare them, and then Junior said he heard the man reload. The man lobbed the shotgun over the fence and then jumped over the fence after it. When he landed, Junior released Nippers who was all over him before he could reach the shotgun. Then Junior opened the gate from the inside and let the hounds in. Because the man still had the T-shirt inside his jacket, the hounds attacked him with Nippers and pretty much tore him to pieces. Junior wiped off Nippers's mouth and put him back in the house, he said, and then locked the gate and left. The man was unconscious with his hounds standing next to him, panting with blood still on their muzzles. They were whining a little, probably realizing their mistake.

We all kept looking toward the Cannolis, then back at Junior. His tales were sometimes too tall to climb without a rope, but this one had a certain feel of truth to it.

"How's Blue Boy?" Junior asked.

"Still alive and well," Bill Loon said, reeling quickly and then stopping for a few seconds so the kite wouldn't do a deep loop.

"Better than daddy. Hey little General, why don't you go over and turn his pickup off?" he said to me. "I don't think Pop Scuttles is going to need it anymore today."

Sherry and I walked over to the truck. I reached inside and turned the key off. The engine stopped. All we could hear now were the cheers of the kids as Kirk came closer to the ground and the sounds of the seagulls circling around the Flying Boxcar. We looked at each other and pretended to ourselves like we were kissing. We wouldn't do it for real with everyone able to look right over, even though they weren't. Sherry reached under my jacket and pulled me to her a little bit. That would be enough for right now. We walked back to the group, whose eyes were still focused on the kite. I realized that no one cared anymore if we were in love or not. It was old news now. I looked over at Sherry and she smiled. She cared. That was plenty.

"Hey, Little Billy Goat Gruff! The troll is down for the count!" Junior shouted up to Kirk as he neared the ground.

In a few minutes the Flying Boxcar hit the lupines coming in at a bad angle and broke apart with Kirk hanging upside down. Bill Loon and Junior quickly got him untied and out of it, and he was chattering and shaking from the cold, but he was fine.

"That was the gr-greatest ride. For a while I was thinkin' that I was in that c-coronation funeral in New Orleans. I was g-goin' to be the dead guy I saw that day and all of you down here would be playin' trumpets and stuff. If it wudn't for the hot ch-chocolate and blanket I'd a froze sure."

"The wind plays tricks on your mind sometimes," Bill Loon said. "It makes you think things that aren't true."

"It plays tricks on your innards too," Kirk said as he suddenly fell to the ground, unable to stand. His legs were shaking uncontrollably. "It'll flat freeze a liver."

He tried to rub his legs to get them to stop shaking, but he couldn't.

"Here let us do that," Sherry said, smiling at Mary Ann. They put their hands inside his clothes to get him warm. His face jumped as his eyes shot in all directions at once. He giggled, hacked a little cough and rolled around with them, until he started to get warm. Mary Ann kept trying to correct his funny English, but it was hopeless. That's just the way he talked. All the time he kept claiming that he was the luckiest boy in the world and this was his luckiest day ever.

We finally noticed a few people starting to come out of their houses with coffee cups as they usually did a little before noon. All the adults seemed to sleep in on Saturday, because they usually stayed up late Friday night. They would often come to see the kites in the air, but fortunately this time they were too late to see Kirk's flight over Humboldt Bay.

"Was that a shotgun blast?" a couple of adults asked.

"That's what we heard," Junior said right away. "It came from the Cannolis'. Maybe somebody ought to go check."

Kirk eventually managed to stand and said he had finally done something really different like he always wanted to do, instead of just being something really different. It was all thanks to his new friends who had to be the nuttiest nut people in the world. Nuttier than anything in New Orleans, he claimed. He said we saved his life and made it look easy.

"Easy?" Bill Loon and Junior Malstrom said. It was the only time I ever heard them say the same word together.

"What if this is the best dang day I ever have in my life? It might'n be y'know," Kirk said, walking a few steps with the small blanket around him.

We all made a pact that no one would ever tell anyone what had happened. All we knew was a man parked his truck on the hog fuel road near where we were flying kites and then walked toward the Cannolis' with his dogs. We thought he was out hunting rabbits. When we heard two shotgun blasts, we just figured he had killed a rabbit. We didn't leave, because we had our kites in the air. All the kids agreed to never mention that we had put a kid from Blue Hollar, Georgia, up in a kite over Humboldt Bay. Some younger kids broke the pact, of course, after a few weeks. But nobody over twenty years old ever believed them. A few of them even got lickings for lying.

Too cracked into pieces to be repaired, the Flying Boxcar never went into the air again. We had a little bonfire that night. We drank hot chocolate and watched it go up in smoke. Bill Loon told us for his own sake it was probably better that we just forget what happened that day and even forget there was ever such a thing as the Flying Boxcar. That way he wouldn't get into trouble. We agreed, of course, but we couldn't forget what happened. We just referred to that morning as Blue Saturday and never said anything about it except to ourselves. In spite of the gossip that went around town, we all knew what had really happened, and because it did, we knew inside that just about anything in the world is possible.

❡

There was a newspaper story in the morning *Eureka Times* the next day. Most of the actual facts were wrong or missing, of course, and the ones that were included were either screwed up or made up, but it was still an interesting story.

The headline read:

> Hunting Dogs Held
> In Bite-and-
> Switch Attack

The subhead read:

> Burglar in Coma After
> Attack By Own Dogs
> Not Expected to Live

The story read:

> Fairhaven, Saturday. An armed burglary attempt was inadvertently thwarted when a burglar's own dogs attacked and nearly killed him for no apparent reason. The event occurred at the John Cannoli residence in the settlement of Fairhaven on the North Spit of Humboldt Bay at approximately 11:00 a.m. while the family was on vacation. The would-be burglar, identified as Warren Dean Scuttles of Toccoa, Georgia, armed with a 12-gauge shotgun, attempted to gain entry to the house. Two shotgun blasts, fired by Scuttles, apparently in an attempt to stop the attack of his own dogs, were heard by locals including children flying kites in a nearby field. A large Doberman known as "Nippers" owned by the Cannolis was locked inside the home and apparently played no part in

the incident. Scuttles suffered severe head and neck injuries and is not expected to live.

The caretaker of the residence during the Cannolis' absence, fourteen-year-old Waldo "Junior" Malstrom, of Fairhaven, claimed to know nothing of the attempted burglary until after he heard the shotgun blasts while flying kites with the other peninsula children. The two large hunting hounds were ordered to be destroyed by the Humboldt County Court authorities, but Malstrom made an impassioned plea on their behalf.

"With a little help, I feel these dogs will make loving family pets. On behalf of the Malstrom family, I would like to adopt them myself. I want to make them available for community service in locating missing persons and also to use for some emergency attack duty," Malstrom added.

I was over at Bill Loon's house that Sunday afternoon. We were reading the morning newspaper. Mary Ann and Sherry were in the kitchen baking some really good-smelling bread.

"What do you want those dogs for, anyway?" Bill Loon asked Junior as he sorted through his fishing tackle.

"Scuttles said he paid $200 for them. They must be worth something to somebody," Junior said. "It's just a matter of cashing in by finding out who."

"Isn't it by finding out whom?" Mary Ann called from the kitchen and we all laughed, because we didn't know and didn't really care. We said it was up to her to find out. She's the one who wanted to be a school teacher.

The Talent Show

MARCH THROUGH LIFE to a different drummer, and people may not follow, but they will admire you. Sing off-key once, and they will run you off the planet. That's all I know about music. It was the gift I always wanted and never got. It felt as if I got instead an empty gift-wrapped box from the music store window that promised everything at a glance. I could tap it, shake it and take it with me, but when I went to open it up and claim the much wanted gift, there was no melody inside and no clue to finding it.

Nevertheless, I had a quest. By the time I was three years old I was in a band. It was called a rhythm band. A group of kids short on melody, long on heart. Being the youngest member of the group, I played the blocks. Clack clack clack. It sounded like I was locked in an attic. It looked like I was trying to build something with no nails. I wanted to play the tambourine, but the leader said absolutely not. I had to learn to play the blocks right first. *How could I play them wrong?* I thought. There were only two of them. The triangle player said I wasn't really playing them wrong. It was just that I was playing them all the time. I was only supposed to play them when the leader pointed at me. I didn't know that, so I started watching her. She never pointed at me. She said it was too much of a risk. Once I started, she couldn't get me to stop. I told her I would stop if I could play the tambourine. She said no, and I started to scream so she said she would think about it. She let me have one to play-practice for her to see how I did, but she pouted when she watched me. She said to only hit it with the other hand not on my head, my shoulders and knees.

Then one day someone got the measles and I moved up to fourth tambourine. We played on the back of a stake bed truck at parking lots and street corners. A young girl, probably my age, watched me play one day when I forgot I was only supposed to hit the tambourine with the other hand. She had her mother lift her onto the truck so she could kiss me. She held the tambourine for a minute. "Stop playing for a second and say something to me," she said smiling. I said, "Hello, little girl." She smiled again and called out to her mother that I said hello. Her mother smiled too and lifted her back off the truck. They both waved goodbye as the truck drove away. Maybe I would do better with the spoken word. That idea is what I took away from that day.

◉

Years later and miles away, I was sitting on the ground in the hog fuel playground, running the chips of plywood through my fingers. My back was against the wall of Rolph School, a lone building which sat about 100 yards from the shore of Humboldt Bay. Sherry Ferston was inside at the piano and through the open window I could hear her taking a lesson from Miss Nickols. Her music softened and stiffened stuff all at the same time. Softened my heart and stiffened my muscles. That's just the way her music was for me. It wasn't a lesson I was hearing. It was a rush of energy vibrating the wood siding against my shoulders.

My lesson was next. It was an ordeal. A mover trying to coax a piano up four flights of stairs. Sherry's lesson was a melody out of time enjoying a summer's sea breeze. Mine was bad weather. Small craft warnings everywhere. Tense navigating with no port in sight. It wasn't really a lesson because it seemed like I never learned anything. Hers wasn't a lesson either, because it seemed like she already knew it.

Music was the gift I had always wanted, and I knew by now the only way I would ever experience it was to be around someone who was willing to share. Sherry was more than willing. And her gift was as great to me as any music in any seaport town in the world could be. Her good looks only added to the package. Some days when I was getting up, I felt I was the luckiest boy in the world. When I would jump down from my bunk bed, I just knew I would always be lighter than the sun.

After a while what we had was more than music. No one knew how much of each other we were sharing. Not even us. But as time went on, it was a lot. People I'd see would ask me how she was doing or where she was like it was the most normal thing in the world. When someone would mention puppy love, it never bothered Sherry. She told me not to let it bother me either. "Age doesn't mean anything," she would say. "We can't help being how old we are." She was right. I knew it, and knowing it made me stronger.

One time she said, "We work with what we got, little General. And what we got looks good from here." She liked to call me General. It was okay with me. I didn't think I deserved it, and when Junior Malstrom said it I knew he was making fun of me, but it was okay. Another time she whispered, "Don't worry, it'll grow." And then she took off running so fast she was almost to the bay before I caught her. I thought that was a little too personal and I told her so. She said she thought we didn't have long to wait so I let her off the hook.

@

The PTA talent show was the last big event of the school year. With only thirty kids in the school, grades one through six, there was always a struggle to put enough acts together to make it an actual show. Everybody could act up, a few could show off, but it wasn't a performing arts grammar school by any means.

That last year I was in Fairhaven, almost one half of the school consisted of first and second graders who, on a good day, could barely hold hands and stand in a crooked line for a full minute. They were in the west classroom with dull Mrs. Chalmers. We were in the east room with ever alert Miss Nickols. The west classroom could sing "Teensy Weensie Spider," but not without falling over or making their spider grab somebody's nose. In spite of that, Miss Nickols, who was responsible for the event, said that they would open the show with orders from headquarters to keep their hands to themselves.

Charlie Low Eagle, an actual Apache, was willing to do some knife tricks, but Miss Nickols didn't like the idea of stabbing the hardwood floor of the PTA room. He told her that if she was worried about nicking up the floor, he could put a couple of students against the bulletin board and throw knives near the heads. He said he could come close enough to make people in the audience gasp, but he promised to miss the students. His grandfather had actually worked in Buffalo Bill's Wild West Show and had taught him, he told her.

"No, too risky," Miss Nickols said. "I'm sure you would miss them. I trust you Charlie. But somebody might have a heart attack. Like me, as an example." She wanted him in the show because he was an incredible athlete. She thought he reflected the power and potential of the Indian community much the same as Jim Thorpe, Olympic athlete at the turn of the century, had done. If Miss Nickols liked you, she talked it up really big. Could he do anything with a rope? Nope. He could dress a deer, he said, but that was too gory, plus we had no deer on the peninsula.

I said that he could beat up six kids at one time without breaking any bones. He would have them banging into and falling all over each other. Miss Nickols said it was a talent show, not a barroom brawl. Jake Fowler said it didn't matter. We'd never find six volunteers with a death wish. Then Mary Ann remembered Charlie could do one-arm pushups. "He can?" Miss Nickols's face brightened. "What are those? How many can you do?"

"Ten with my right arm. Twenty with my left," Charlie said.

We all knew Charlie was left-handed, but he didn't like to be called Lefty. We called him that once, and that's how we found out he could beat up six kids at one time. Miss Nickols watched as he did the one-arm pushups. She clapped when he was finished. No one else did. We had seen him do it lots of times. She told Sherry to have the announcer say, "From the physical education department here at Rolph School, please welcome Charlie Low Eagle." Then everyone was to circle around him, sitting and patting the floor like it's a drum ceremony and clap when he finishes.

"Can we go woo woo woo, like a war hoop?" Jake Fowler asked.

"No," Miss Nickols said without even looking at him.

Jake Fowler had two jokes he wanted to tell as part of the program. Miss Nickols wanted to hear them. Twice. She wanted to make sure they didn't change. She made him take out two words and switch the locale from a bar to a soda shop. She said if he changed anything in the performance like he did last year, she would fail him and he would be repeating the fifth grade. She didn't want anything out of line in this show. Because of those jokes last year, the ladies of the PTA filed a petition against her with the school board. She got off with a talking-to, but it made her skittish. Nobody in Rolph School knew about that except me and Sherry and Mary Ann. Junior Malstrom told us his dad was drinking and talking about it at dinner one night. His dad was on the school board so he learned a lot about what inner workings were going on at the school.

Sherry Ferston and Mary Ann Loon could sing harmony so well they could do the Andrew sisters' songbook in their sleep. It was just a matter of picking what they wanted to sing for the show. They had been working on some numbers with the big attraction of that year's show, Kirk Odekirk, the story-telling streak from Blue Hollar who was a visual delight with his pure blue-colored skin. He was a small boy from Georgia, almost translucent and seemed like he was born to be on the stage. When he played his musical spoons, it was like a whole percussion section. It reminded me of when I played tambourine in the rhythm band so many years before. He would do some songs with them and then tell some stories in time to his spoons. He said he would tell about being a Penguin Boy in the circus, about being in New Orleans and about the best time he ever had in his life, which was flying over Humboldt Bay in a giant kite. He had done that a few weeks previously in Bill Loon's Flying Boxcar, a kite so large it looked like an open air storage shed.

"Don't do that story," Mary Ann said. "You could get my brother Bill in trouble."

He said he could do it like it was a fairy tale dream that he thought up, so she said she thought that might be all right.

Sherry Ferston had a piano and vocal medley she worked out, which was a group of old favorites. Kirk would play his spoons with some of them; Mary Ann would sing harmony on some and then sing one on her own. With no music to offer, I was mostly hanging around watching rehearsals.

"You sure *look* like you have talent," Sherry said. "Can't you do anything musical?"

"I used to play the tambourine," I said.

"We don't have a tambourine," Mary Ann said.

We are lucky, I thought to myself.

"Well, you can certainly be the announcer," Sherry said. "You don't need a lot of talent for that."

"Announcers have talent," I said. "Plus I can, uh, come here a second." I whispered to Sherry.

"A poem?" She pulled back and looked at me over her pink glasses. "What kind of poem?"

"A ballad, you know, a poem with a story. I know one nobody's ever heard. I learned it just this week and never recited it. It's about a boat cruising down the Mississippi River. These two people are going to get married and a bad guy tries to stop them."

"I don't know," Sherry said. "It sounds kind of serious."

"It is kind of serious. Her father owns the boat," I said.

"Her father owns the boat? We'll have to ask Miss Nickols, but I like it. How long is it?"

"It's sixty feet. Paddle wheeler," I said.

"How long is the poem?" Sherry said.

"Maybe ten minutes. It's a ballad," I said. "Like Longfellow writes."

"Do you know it by heart?" She asked. I nodded. "Wow," she said.

"Mary Ann, Kirk. Listen to this. We do 'Cruising Down the River,' right? In the middle, we hum a little and the General does his 'Longfellow on the Mississippi' boat ballad. Kirk can highlight the poem with his spoons at the end of the verses. When he finishes the poem, they applaud and we start playing 'Cruising Down the River' again for a big last verse, then we all stand and bow."

Sherry pulled me close and whispered in my ear. "You're in the show now, little General. You better be good." She smiled and saluted.

Everything was going so fast. Sherry told Miss Nickols that I was doing something like Henry Wadsworth Longfellow, that I had memorized, and she was so busy she said, "What, Hiawatha? Paul Revere? All of his are fine. It doesn't matter. He can read one. Sure. But what about those first and second graders? They are all over hell's half-acre most of the time."

"Miss Nickols!" someone called out.

"Sorry. Heck's half-acre."

The day of the performance, nearly everyone in Fairhaven showed up. It would have been a good day for burglars. They could have robbed nearly every house in the settlement. People who had no kids were there. Guys from the mill got off early to come. Everyone had been anxious to see the blue boy. They knew about him and word got around that he had been in the circus and was a real performer. It was standing room only by showtime.

I did the announcing. The opening number, which was composed of the first and second graders, started off okay, but quickly degenerated. The "Teensy Weensie Spider," never made it up the spout once. All the kids were pinching each other while they laughed and yelled, "Teensy Weensie on you!" until the whole herd of them had to be shooed offstage like unruly cats.

Charlie Low Eagle saved the show by getting a standing ovation. He not only did one-arm pushups, but left the ground on most of them.

Jake Fowler got laughs. Seeing Miss Nickols in the front row, jaw tight and pencil up, he didn't change a word. When he was nearly finished, he told the audience that the jokes would have been better, but Miss Nickols made him take out the good parts. He got his biggest laugh at that. He was a natural comedian.

Sherry and Mary Ann had flowers in their hair as they walked into the room. They sang like angels. Kirk walked in and around them like Cupid in a candy shop. Sherry was stunning. She was so beautiful I almost forgot my poem. I thought she looked just like the daughter of a very lucky riverboat captain.

Kirk sat on a small stool and told the story about him being the Penguin Boy in the circus and the one about being in a funeral parade in New Orleans, and then he told about being up in the kite over Humboldt Bay. He said it was a dream, but when he finished he said it was so real, it seemed to him like it really happened. Then he mentioned the Flying Boxcar and the audience was beginning to believe it really had happened. They were asking each other, "Is that true?" "Did they put him up in a kite?" "I wouldn't put it past the little hooligans." "I heard they raced a horse against a car." We were sweating bullets. Then he started talking about how all the kids in Fairhaven had accepted him so well that he thought this was the best school and the best town he had ever been in. He got a standing ovation and he bowed and gave a big spoon roll while Sherry and Mary Ann started singing "Cruising down the River" in harmony. Everyone got sentimental and rocking to and fro and Kirk gave a little accent from time to time with the spoons. He announced me the way we had planned.

"And now General George Armstrong Custer will give you a riverboat saga in the fine southern tradition of Robert E. Longfellow." Everyone smiled and clapped. Sherry made the song sound a little like ragtime and pretty soon it was like we were actually on a riverboat.

I came out with a cowboy hat on my finger, smiled at Sherry, nodded to Kirk on his small stool and said first to them and then to the audience, "Derringer Dan was a gamblin' man who plied his trade on the Nellie Bly / whose paddles dipped in the Mississip as the swampy banks slid by. / The backs he rimmed as the cards he skimmed with never a crooked move. / Early and late he shuffled them straight for his heart held naught but love." I put the hat on and walked over to Sherry who was playing the piano softly. She became the captain's daughter in the mind of the audience. "The guiding force that mapped his course was his sweetheart Natchez Nan, / the captain's daughter who loved the water and worshipped Derringer Dan." I looked at Sherry again, and she blew me a kiss. "The whistle blew for the Belle Bayou with its landings, piles and bales. / The lusty shout of the roust-abouts answered by the planter's hails . . ."

"That's not Longfellow," I heard the PTA president say to Miss Nickols. "And there's no Robert E. Longfellow either. It's Henry Wadsworth Longfellow." Miss Nickols had to agree, but then I never said it was Longfellow. I said it was like Longfellow. I didn't even know who wrote it, but I liked it and I thought other people would too. It was a lot easier than trying to make people like my tambourine playing even if we had one.

"Handsome Hank strolled up the plank, a pearler, rake and scamp. / A low-life robber and a poker dauber from an upstate mussel camp," I continued. I could feel the tension. Then when I said "He bartered his pearls with the crib line girls at Natchez-Under-the-Hill," some of the lumbermen burst out cheering. But not for long. Some of their wives hit them with their fists and purses. There was turmoil in the audience now, not just tension.

I knew the poem was good; I didn't realize it was pure dynamite until right at that moment.

Miss Nickols was starting to get her hives while she tried to quiet everyone down. The room was heating up. I continued. Dan accuses Hank of cheating and Hank shoots him and then Nan takes Dan's pistol, which was evidently an old cap and ball type, because the poem says that "She slammed a ball through the cabin wall / and through the heart of the pearler man." I realized when the men cheered again that it sounded like she slammed *his balls* through the cabin wall, which was not the case, but it was too late. You can't stop in the middle of the poem to explain. I kept going. Sherry kept playing and Kirk kept clicking his spoons. We paddled through the troubled waters and by the time the end of the poem came, Dan was dead, Hank was dead, and "The captain's daughter who loved the water" had "hopped into the Mississip." A double murder and suicide right there in Fairhaven and at the PTA meeting to boot. I hadn't thought about it that way before I did it. At first it was totally quiet, except for the sublime harmony of Sherry and Mary Ann who were finishing the last lines of "Cruising Down the River on a Sunday Afternoon."

Then there was total silence, and then a sudden burst of applause and shouting, mostly from the lumbermen to start with and then it seemed like everyone was clapping. "More. More!"

We all took a bow. Charlie Low Eagle and Jake Fowler joined us. Each of us came forward individually, and everyone clapped even more. Charlie hoisted Kirk on his shoulder with one hand and it was obvious from the applause that he was the favorite. Finally the first and second graders were let back in the room, and we all bowed one last time. Sherry pulled me to the side and whispered something in my ear something so simple and full of power that I never forgot it. Then the show was over. But the trouble was just beginning.

Ten minutes later, the four of us were standing at Miss Nickols's desk. No one had heard the ballad before the show except me. So she said if that was the case, everyone else could leave. But Sherry wouldn't go. She said she was the one who told her it was like Longfellow so she was staying. Mary Ann said she was staying if Sherry was. They did everything together. Then she looked at me. "Almost everything," she added.

Kirk said, "I've been in trouble most of my life, Miz Nickel, until I arrived on your fair shores. I gotta say I'm glad this all happened. I was plumb out of practice."

Miss Nickols shook her head and hid her face so we wouldn't know she was trying to keep from splitting apart laughing. Finally she looked up sternly. "What is your father going to say, Sherry? And what about yours, Randy Ray McKenzie?" I hated when she said my full name. It was like somebody taking your pants down in front of everybody.

My dad had not seen the show, but he was called over and had a private talk with Miss Nickols. All I heard through the transom was, "He doesn't know what a crib line girl is? It's not my fault. I tried to teach him."

Sherry's father, who had seen the show, said it was a little strong for a PTA meeting, but it was the best show they ever had. The mill workers loved it and were making a large contribution to the PTA treasury. That shut up the founding mothers of the organization very quickly so Miss Nickols never had any repercussions like she had the year before with Jake Fowler's jokes.

Miss Nickols asked Sherry's father if he wasn't worried about Sherry's reputation by acting like a riverboat piano player and hanging out with me alone a lot after school, which seemed to be common knowledge. I cringed a little. He said he wasn't worried about her reputation. She could whip her weight in wildcats and correct any rumors. He was probably right there. Just before he left he said, "You four were some real humdingers."

"Your pap's a dang sight better'n mine ever was," Kirk said to Sherry and smiled. Junior Malstrom's father came over to the school the next day and said he heard it was a good show, could they do it again? Miss Nickols answered simply, "No."

@

We did most of the show once again anyway that Saturday at the Ferston house for a crab boil they had. It was a hit all over again. Even more people came because it was in the evening. There was plenty of drink and food for everyone, so they stayed late. Sherry and I sat on the front porch swing, looked up at the stars and watched the adults drinking and playing.

"Do you think someday we will be like that?" Sherry asked.

"I don't think so now," I said. "But I could be wrong."

It turned out I was right. I didn't know it that night, but in a few weeks, we would be moving from Fairhaven. I would only see Sherry once more in my life, the following year when my family stopped in to visit the former neighbors in Fairhaven on vacation. We didn't have too much time to be together alone, but we walked out behind her house and held hands for a little while. We still kind of connected the way we used to, but we were a little older now and there was nothing we could do about it. My only contact with her after that was the letters she sent during high school and one or two after I started college and then those stopped. The last one I got was from Saigon. The last line read: "Love from another unlikely seaport town, Sherry."

@

All I could really do after that was to go back to Fairhaven the next summer to see her dad, see the pictures of her in her uniform and listen to him quietly tell how she died. All that music, all that toughness and beauty. My God, First Lieutenant Sherry Ferston, United States Army, was gone. I was in my second year of college when her music simply stopped.

"It wasn't really Combat Nurse," her dad told me. "It was just the medical corps. It's just what she liked to call it, and then she'd laugh. You're the one she always called the General, aren't you? Why was that, Randy?"

"It started out as a joke," I said. "And kind of caught on. Kid stuff. It was a long time ago. Nobody remembers now."

"You and that Loon girl and the blue kid. I can remember it like it was today. What an act that was. And that powerhouse Indian boy and the kid with the jokes. You made a goddam perfect world up there that day in the PTA room. There was something for everybody and you delivered it right in their laps. We don't have that Rolph School anymore, you know. Closed it. The kids get bussed to town now."

I remembered again what Sherry had whispered when she hugged me and kissed me on the ear just after the show. "Life and music. It's always so good when it happens, isn't it? That's all we really need to know."

Sherry Ferston was right. Life in Fairhaven was good when it was happening. She was the music, and that's all I need to know.

Biographical Note

A Southern California native, businessman Brad Wethern is a Cal Berkeley graduate. An actor for several years in San Francisco, New York, and Chicago, he returned to California to go into business as a real estate agent. He has recently appeared as a regular on the KVCR TV show *Voice of the Inland Empire*. Additionally, he appears as a motivational speaker on a regular basis at the Claremont Center for Spiritual Living. He has two grown children and makes his home in Ontario, California.